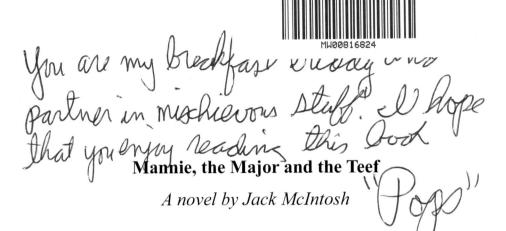

You are my breakfast buddy and partner in mischievous stuff. I hope that you enjoy reading this book

Mannie, the Major and the Teef

A novel by Jack McIntosh

"Pops"

Jack McIntosh

EVENING POST BOOKS
Our Accent Is Southern!

McIntosh, Jack. Mannie, the Major, and the Teef

Published by Evening Post Books, Charleston, South Carolina.

ISBN-13: 978-1-929647-61-3

Cover illustration Robert Ariail

Interior design Michael J. Nolan

 **Jack McIntosh** grew up on Chapel Street on the Cooper River side of Charleston, South Carolina and attended public school. He finished high school in 1945 and served three years in the US Marine Corps and used the G.I. Bill to attend Furman University, graduating in 1952. While at Furman he helped establish the ROTC program and served as the first Cadet Colonel. He was called again to active duty in the Army and served as a tank platoon leader in Korea. When the conflict ended, he attended law school at the University of South Carolina and graduated in 1956. He retired after fifty years of practice in Anderson, South Carolina and enjoys his new career as a writer.

Mannie, The Major, and the Teef is his first novel following two humorous books, *Dont Kill All the Lawyers…I'll give you a short list*, and *Ain't Mad at Nobody*. He published a biography of his friend and classmate at Furman, Frank Selvey, titled *The Coal Miner's Son*.

Entering a new career as a writer was made possible by his friend and mentor, Kathryn Smith.

 **Robert Ariail** (cover illustrtation) is a longtime South Carolina editorial cartoonist. His work is nationally syndicated to over 600 newspapers and has won numerous national, regional and state awards. Ariail was also awarded the Elizabeth O'Neill Verner Governor's Award for the Arts, and he has been a finalist for The Pulitzer Prize three times. Robert has had the pleasure of illustrating two previous books by Jack McIntosh.

Dedication

I dedicate this book to my comrades who have worn the globe and eagle and embraced the slogan *semper fidelis*. To the same extent I include those who have served in the Army, Navy, Air Force, and Coast Guard. For those who gave their lives, as did my first cousin PFC Charles McIntosh at Guadalcanal — fresh from the farm and eighteen years old — I call on every American to reserve their pedestals for these special heroes.

Chapter 1

Mannie Simmons

The young man drove the small Ford slowly down the cobble-stone street on a warm afternoon in the spring of 1945. There were two good reasons he drove slowly on Chapel Street: the cobblestones for one, and the fact that he was looking for an address for another. The stones that paved Chapel Street were set in a pattern using smooth Belgian blocks, which were uniformly arranged on both sides with round cobblestones providing a contrast along the center of the wide street. A railroad track extended along the south side leading from the waterfront on the east to a point on John Street where it veered off and headed north out of town.

There was an interesting variety of houses on Chapel Street, ranging from those that had once been mansion houses with slave quarters in the rear to less pretentious framed houses located on deep, narrow lots. The house he was looking for was back off the street behind the big house at 34 Chapel, a former mansion that had been converted into apartments and was beginning to show the effects of years of overuse. The war effort had brought many defense workers into the city, all of them looking for something to rent. Like most tenants, they weren't inclined to maintain a rented place and, even if they were, there was a shortage of building materials and workmen. If you couldn't fix it yourself, it probably didn't get fixed.

That was over now, at least part of it was. Germany had surrendered on May 8, but the Japanese were still fighting, and despite losing a string of island engagements with the Marines and Army and big sea battles with the Navy, they still showed no sign of giving in. They were at the fanatical phase of the war where they sent young fliers on kamikaze missions which were causing a lot of damage to American ships.

There had always been a lot of discussion about the Japanese, but it related mostly to the invasion of China and the atrocities committed there. Americans saw them as comical characters and said that we could beat them with one hand tied behind our back. Then came Pearl Harbor. Much had been learned during the bloody fighting in the Pacific, but everyone in Charleston felt optimistic that "our" boys and men would be coming home soon, and the hard times would be over.

The young man finally arrived at 34 Chapel and a little boy directed him to the alleyway running beside the big house. It led to the former slave quarters and carriage house located in the rear. He parked the car and walked down the alley to the home of Manigault Simmons.

Mannie lived upstairs over the carriage house and stabled his horse down below in the former garage area. It was all comfortably arranged. The horse's stall was spacious, with fresh straw underfoot and plenty of hay in the trough. The yard was swept and neat with a few flower beds around. A chicken pen with coops and roosts was in a corner of the yard and the red chickens were contentedly clucking and scratching around in the dirt.

How unusual, thought the young man, a reporter from the *News and Courier*, as he looked around for the subject of his assignment. It's like stepping back in time. He turned to look at the long shed where he heard a noise and saw an elderly black man coming out of an enclosed area.

"How do you do?" he asked

"I'm fine. Can I help you?" asked the old man.

"I'll bet you're Mannie Simmons."

"How much do you want to bet?" asked the man, breaking into a smile.

"Well, I don't want to bet at all but if I did, I would bet that you're Mannie Simmons," replied the reporter.

"And you'd be right!" laughed the man.

"I'm a reporter from the *News and Courier*. I want to ask you some questions."

"I can't imagine what the *News and Courier* would want from me," said Mannie.

"My editor thought it unusual that Major Frank Manigault left you some valuable property in his will. He thought it would make a good human-interest piece."

"Well, son, Frank Manigault probably wouldn't want it made into a story," Mannie replied, shaking his head. "He never wanted publicity while he was alive, and I don't think his family would want it now. You check with his widow and if she agrees, I'll talk with you."

The reporter was prepared. "We already have. We asked her why you were in his will and she said to ask you. She obviously likes you and said it was alright with the family for you to tell the story if you wanted to."

"It's funny how you get yourself tied up in other people's lives," the old man said after a long pause during which he went to the stall and led his horse out and proceeded to rub him down with a soft brush. He stopped rubbing the horse, turned and looked at the reporter and said, "You want to know why Frank Manigault put me in his will. You'll probably want to know about Tee Mc-Lauren too. Well, I can only tell you that Frank had many friends and I was lucky enough to be one of them. He was my friend and that should be enough to answer your question."

The reporter thought a moment as he studied the face of the old man and then said, "Don't you agree that your friendship was unusual?"

"I guess so but that would also apply to Tee McLauren, they were also friends," Mannie replied over his shoulder; he had gone back to rubbing down the horse.

"How did you become friends?" the reporter persisted.

"Frank said it was a Presbyterian thing, but I didn't. No, I don't blame God for things that happen in our lives, so I don't blame God for putting us together. The fact is our paths crossed as we went about the business of living. We just hooked up together by accident, I suppose; we sure had different backgrounds." He paused and looked off in the distance and in a softer voice he said, "Presbyterian," and laughed.

"I've lived alone since my wife died," he continued. "I enjoyed her company and we read and talked a lot. I've always enjoyed good, intelligent conversation, which she and I had. The Major was a highly educated and intelligent man with a quick wit and a taste for good food and good spirits. Truth is, we just got to like each other, and we helped each other sometimes. I don't reckon it's too strange. I guess if you spend time together most people could be friends," the old man continued as he stroked his old horse on the head and hand-fed him some sweet oats and corn. He said quietly, almost as if talking to the horse, "I miss my wife and I miss my old friend."

"You don't seem to think it's unusual," said the reporter, "but my editor sees a story here. Here's a friendship between a rich old Huguenot and a poor produce vendor. Your first name is the same as his last name...Manigault. Somewhere back your family was probably his family's slaves. Do you suppose that was the case?"

"I don't suppose that, but I think you do," Mannie said with a grin. "You hope so anyway because it would make a good story. Well, I hate to disappoint you but that's not how it was. For one thing, I'm not poor. He didn't remember me in his will because he thought I was poor; he knew different. Some of his ancestors had slaves, like most well-off people around here, but I know they weren't traders. Yeah, they had slaves alright, but so did mine." The old man turned from tending to the horse and looked straight at the reporter and laughed openly at the surprised look on his face.

"Yes, he and I both came from slave holders. Some of his family had slaves. My family worked both sides of the street; they started out as plantation slaves and when the Simmons family brought them to the city my ancestor worked under a permit as a carpenter and made enough to buy them out. Old man Simmons was a good fellow and was more than fair for that time."

"You mean that your ancestor then bought slaves himself?"

"Yes, that's what I mean. He wasn't a trader either, but he bought some and he freed some. He opened a shop and went in business doing all kinds of carpentry work. He even made good furniture and sold it. He trained a lot of workers and gave them a chance to buy out, which some of them did. This is some of the stuff Frank and I talked about, but there was a lot more."

"How did your ancestor become a carpenter? I thought slaves

worked in the fields picking cotton and things like that," said the reporter.

"You need to read some history, South Carolina history," Mannie said. "When you do, you'll learn a lot about plantations and slaves. The slaves built those great plantation homes and much of the furniture you find in them. They learned to do all kinds of things that were necessary to run the business of the plantation. Some of them became really good at their craft, like my ancestor."

"I guess so," said the reporter, then, more quietly, "Of course they would," obviously thinking over what he had just heard. After a pause he said, "So, the two of you had a sort of social club? Tell me about it."

"Well, let's introduce ourselves first. What's your name?"

"George Johnson," the young man replied, and extended his hand.

After a good, firm handshake, Mannie said, "There were three of us. Frank Manigault lived on the route where I sold vegetables and seafood from my wagon and had a good eye for produce. He would come down to the wagon and pick over the vegetables and other things. I started putting things aside for him and he liked that. He was a good cook and liked to experiment with things and so did I. We started out exchanging recipes. I was doing a fish one evening and I invited him over to my yard to try it out and it sort of became a monthly thing. He would cook and I would cook, and we would sometimes cook together. We shared the expenses. Good food and a little wine led to good conversations. That's how we became friends."

"But you said there were three of you."

"Yes. Tee McLauren was the third."

"He was a young criminal who did some time at Florence, wasn't he?" asked George suspiciously.

"Well, it looks like you started asking around before you came here, I guess. I guarantee you didn't get accurate information, or you would know he was a lot more than that. We'll need to talk about him. Yeah, he was a lot more than that," Mannie said.

"Did you ever go to Mr. Manigault's house?"

"Well, he was a customer of mine and I was a client of his; he was in the investment business. You might say we worked for each other. I delivered produce to his home. I even did some work for him. He showed me all through the house; it's a grand house. I met his family and they're nice people. Son, it's no big mystery here, our worlds touched but they didn't merge. I suspect that you have people you enjoy at work who you don't invite to do other things. Enjoy what's comfortable and don't push things. I tell you what, why don't you get yourself a cup of my world-class coffee and a ham biscuit and relax yourself while I finish with taking care of my other old friend and I'll tell you about Tee McLauren: he's the story. I'll start in the winter of 1941 when I introduced him to Frank…Oh, and by the way, don't be taking notes while I talk, it makes me feel unnatural."

Mannie put the horse in the stable, poured cups of coffee and produced ham biscuits for himself and his guest. He sat down in the cracked leather sofa, which his friend Frank had brought to the shed along with the matching chair the young man was laid back in. As they sipped and munched, he paused a good while and smiled as he recalled the story, then he looked off and started to talk.

Chapter 2

Tee McLauren

The Coast Line train from Florence pulled into the Union
Station at Columbus and East Bay Streets. Among the few
passengers who got off was a young man named Tom McLauren, Jr., who went by the name of Tee. He had been released
from the reformatory at Florence that morning, but it took all
day before they got the paperwork done and he was allowed
to leave. It was one o'clock in the morning, several hours since
the warden had given him a ticket and, after a long wait in the
station, he had finally boarded the Coast Line train and made
the trip to Charleston. It was a slow ride as the train made frequent stops at rural stations picking up or throwing off bundles
or bags. It had taken about three hours to travel sixty miles,
but this didn't matter much to Tee, who was glad to be out and
breathing free air.

It was a cold midwinter night, with a frozen mist falling on
anyone unlucky enough to be out. When Tee left the station, he
walked down the middle of the street with the strap of a cloth
bag crossing his shoulder. Everything he owned was either in the

bag or in the pockets of his rain-soaked corduroy pants. He was alone on the street.

Tee looked into an all-night café with its empty booths and counters. He smiled to himself as he watched the old Greek pour water into the coffee maker and wipe the counter. The counter was clean, but this was obviously a routine he followed when he found himself with nothing else to do. The old man appeared pleased to see the boy; he grinned and gave a friendly wave, expecting him to come in, but Tee just smiled, returned the wave, and then walked into the dark street. The man propped his elbows on the counter and continued to gaze in the direction of the boy who would disappear into the night only to reappear each time he came under the circle of light cast down by another streetlight. The old Greek subconsciously amused himself by counting the seconds between lights and could time each appearance of the rain-soaked figure, which like a mechanical silhouette moved predictably into each island of light and then back again behind a wet curtain of darkness. When the figure didn't appear under the next light, he knew the boy had turned off East Bay Street and into the east side.

The rain soaked into Tee's knitted cap and began to run down his neck and back as he walked, but he made no attempt to either avoid it or wipe it away. He didn't seem to notice it or to be uncomfortable because of it. He kept a steady pace for the twenty minutes it took to reach the familiar cobblestones of Chapel Street, continuing to walk in the middle of the street. He felt his shoes slip on the cobblestones, which were slick from years of wear, but he had walked on those stones many times. He stepped up his pace as he came to the alleyway leading to the old slave quarters and stables, which had served the big house at one time but were now the home of Mannie Simmons and his animals.

He moved quietly into the old carriage house, which Mannie

had turned into a stall, rubbed the hard head of the horse, took some dry clothes from the bag, and made himself a comfortable bed on the hay bales. A big dog came in quietly and welcomed him by rubbing against the boy's leg. Tee stroked the dog after he finished with the horse and then pulled an old blanket over his body, head and all; he fell immediately into a deep and quiet sleep. The dog went back under the kitchen shed where he slept. A cat had observed all of this from a distance and had seen no need to get involved.

Tee wasn't sure exactly what it was that woke him up; the coffee, the bacon, or maybe the cat walking over his head, but he opened his eyes to see Mannie Simmons fixing breakfast and looking at him through kind eyes. Tee smiled back at the friendly face and got out of bed already fully dressed and eager to get a better look at his friend and what he knew would be a good meal, and his first one in over twenty-four hours. Longer than that really, because the food at Florence wasn't anything to brag about.

"Well, you got back," said Mannie as he handed over a cup of black coffee in a chipped café mug with no handle. "I was looking for you all day yesterday. Your daddy left the key to your room and a couple of dollars for you before he left. He said he wrote you a card. You know he went back to sea?"

"Yessir, I got the card, but I was late getting on the train and I didn't want to wake you up last night," said the boy. "I was thinking about them hay bales all the way from the station and was glad to get outta the rain. You was sleeping, so I just covered up and died."

Mannie replied, "The wine and conversation flowed last night so I slept pretty soundly. Frank Manigault is coming over in a minute, but you don't have to wait. Get your plate and get over here to the table while I fry you a couple of yard-fresh eggs. You timed this real good. Frank and I cooked last night and decided that since you were coming that we would have a good feed this morning in your honor. He'll be here in a minute and wants to meet you."

Tee knew who Major Manigault was but right now his interest was fixed on biscuits, bacon and eggs and he could only smile around well-stuffed jaws when the old gentleman walked down the alley, sat down across from the boy, smiled, and said to Mannie, "Looks like the prodigal has returned and you've killed the fatted pig. Put a robe and a ring on him and let's hear how it was in the juvenile slammer."

"Major Frank Manigault, meet Thomas McLauren, Jr.," said Mannie. "Folks call him Tee, and you're right, He's probably a hardened criminal now that he's been to crime school. They tell me it's like being an apprentice where you learn a trade. I bet he's planning a bank job right now. Well, not right now. Not till he finishes breakfast. They probably taught him not to rob a bank on an empty stomach."

Tee was happy now. Mannie was a good friend and he liked Major Manigault on the spot. Yes sir, warm food, good friends, and he wasn't mad at anybody. He hadn't felt this good in a long time and wondered how he got so lucky.

"Besides," said Mannie, "they couldn't teach him anything up there. He could teach them a thing or two. I bet they don't know the difference between a thief and a teef." He winked at Tee as he spoke.

"I don't either," said the Major.

Mannie put down his knife and fork, put both elbows on the table, and with a merry face said, "Let the education begin."

Chapter 3

The Teef

It was a Saturday in the fall of 1939 that Mannie had hitched his horse to the wagon and did some hauling for a friend from his church who was moving. She was a member of his choir. It wasn't unusual for him to do some hauling and especially for someone in his church choir. Mannie liked to sing. He sang a lot as he worked. His voice was deep and strong and was somewhere between bass and baritone.

He finished his day and went down to the dock and arranged to pick up some shrimp and crabs to sell from the wagon when he worked his vegetable route on Monday. He got that done and picked up a few things for himself and headed the old horse down the cobblestones on Chapel Street, going slow because the old horse didn't like to move fast, and to keep the cobblestones from shaking the wheels off the old wagon. That was when he got his first glimpse of Tee, who had hopped up on the back of the wagon.

The hitchhiker smiled at Mannie when their eyes met. He had just turned sixteen at the time and was big for his age. He also had a look about him that told you he wasn't just a boy. When the wagon reached 34 Chapel, Mannie made a sharp right into the alleyway running beside the big house, which led to his business and residence. When he stopped and got off, he turned and saw the young boy standing beside the wagon.

"What you want, boy?" asked Mannie, who didn't mind having a non-paying passenger but thought the boy would have gotten off when he turned down the alley. He didn't welcome a guest to his living quarters where he and his horse lived with his cat and dog and a few Rhode Island Red chickens. They had a long-established routine, which didn't include a sixteen-year-old white boy who looked like he might be up to something.

Tee smiled again at the man and walked around the wagon and patted the dog on the head before he proceeded to unhitch the horse. He took the bit out of his mouth and fed him a carrot that he had lifted from Mannie's basket.

"I've got a plan I know you'll like, and I'll explain it to you as soon as I get this old fella free and comfortable," the boy said over his shoulder as he led the horse out of the traces and began to rub him down with a brush and towel he found on the table by the stable.

Mannie picked up his basket from the wagon and walked over to the cooking shed where he unpacked his goods and put the seafood on ice. When that was done, he put on a pot of coffee. This too was a part of his routine, but it usually happened after he had unhitched and stabled the horse himself. He settled himself in the peeled and cracked leather of his favorite stuffed sofa and watched the boy coddle his old animal while he waited for the coffee and enjoyed a pipe of Prince Albert.

After he finished stroking the horse, Tee found the bin where Mannie kept some sweet oats and corn and served a generous helping to the animal, who moved his head happily and nuzzled his new friend.

"You sure are generous with other people's stuff. First you steal a carrot outta my basket then you act like oats and corn grow on trees," Mannie complained, but without anger.

"I know where these things come from," said the boy. "I also know they don't grow on trees, but they do grow, and a wagon is a heavy thing for an old horse to pull. I'm from the country and I know how oats and corn grow and I know when a good horse needs a good meal," he added, continuing to smile at his host.

The coffee was ready, and Mannie put two cupfuls on the table along with two biscuits and some cheese and sat down with this strange boy who was nice and friendly but a little bit pushy. He waited to hear his proposal.

The story of how he met Tee was put on hold for a minute as Major Manigault went over to the stove and served himself more of the coarse ground grits and more of the eggs and bacon. He put some food on the plates of his two companions and then sat down to hear more, still not knowing the difference between a thief and a teef.

Mannie picked up the tale where he left off:

"This horse needs to graze on some pasture grass and you ain't got none here. There's plenty of it on the railroad property growing all around the junk piles," the boy explained while cutting open a biscuit and slicing off a big hunk of cheese.

"I know all about that grass and I know all about the railroad. They don't want anybody on their property, and they'll put you in court if they catch you down there," Mannie replied.

"I thought about that," said Tee. "You don't have to go on their property. I will. I'll take your horse and stake him out in a good place in the middle of a bunch of junk. The detectives don't come down there on Saturday or Sunday, and even if they do, they won't wander into the junk piles. Besides, if the horse eats the grass, it will cut down on the fires they have all the time. We'll be doing them a favor."

Mannie laughed. "You might call it that, but they won't. They'll call it trespass and come after me."

"But you won't be there, and they can't blame you if somebody took your horse and put it down there," the young man argued. "I'll ride him down there on Saturday morning and put him in the place I've fixed up. I'll do it when you go to the docks and I'll bring him back before dark. For a dollar a week I'll put your horse in the pasture and I'll rub him down three times a week."

"You wanna be a horse thief?" asked the old man.

"It ain't stealing," argued the boy. "It's teefin'. Ain't nobody getting hurt and everybody gets something they need. The horse needs the grass, I need the dollar, and the railroad don't need that grass. It balances out," he concluded.

"You're one of them boys what's been stealing junk from the big scrap pile, ain't you?" Mannie asked.

"We don't take enough to make a difference. All the boys around here pick up picture show money that way. We don't think it's a crime to sell junk."

"They ain't gonna see it that way and if they catch you, they'll make an example out of you to scare your friends off," Mannie warned.

"They ain't my friends. I like them OK, but I don't have time to play ball and hang out with them."

Mannie answered, "I'll pay you a dollar a week to take care of my horse and if you want to ride him down to the railroad lot it's OK but be careful. I don't want my horse to get hurt."

"The horse'll like that," the boy responded enthusiastically. "Nobody gets hurt; I get a dollar a week, the horse gets the grass, and we help the railroad by thinning out the grass that causes brush fires."

"Ha! Ha! Ha!" the Major laughed, interrupting the story. "Did you make that argument to the juvenile judge before they sent you to the school?"

"No sir, they got me for selling junk," Tee said. "It was different."

"No son, they didn't get you for selling junk. They got you for stealing junk," the Major said. "The railroad might not want the grass, but they can't let you steal junk from their lot. It doesn't belong to them, but they've been paid to haul it and keep it on the lot until it's moved."

"Well, that's true," said Mannie, "but we all remember when old man Thompson moved to Chapel Street from the Upstate and how we were amused with his accent. He had his eyes on the Japanese from the start and talked about 'Jay-pan.' We thought it was funny when he emphasized the 'Jay' in 'Jay-pan.' It's no longer funny now that they joined up with Germany and Italy in the Axis and have set out to dominate the world. Tee should get a medal." They all laughed, including Tee. Whether it was thieving or teefin' was open to discussion. Tee knew, however, that it wasn't an act of patriotism that led him to the junk pile.

The Major sat quietly looking at this unusual young man, then broke the silence:

"We don't have to decide about the junk, the judge already settled that; he said it was stealing. The thing about the grass, though, is different. He wasn't planning to steal the grass and they weren't planning to give it to him. It was a nuisance and a public hazard with no real value, but he would have to trespass to get it. Trespassing in a hobo jungle isn't much of a crime, I guess, and if it is, it's committed on an ongoing basis by every bum and hobo in the city. Yes, teefin' just might be the proper word for it."

After a lengthy discussion of the pros and cons of teefin', the conversation turned to a discussion of the war in Europe. It was Hitler they were afraid of. You could pick up the broadcasts of the rallies and the frenetic speeches and lusty *Sieg heil* responses of the crowds were frightening, even to an old soldier like Major Manigault. Maybe especially to someone who had faced the Huns in the trenches of the Western Front in France in the Great War as he had, because he knew where such fanaticism led people and the ultimate price they would pay. Neville Chamberlain had gone to the table with good humanitarian arguments and left the meeting feeling that he had preserved the peace only to learn very shortly that the despot had no intention of keeping his promises. Now only England was standing against the dictator, with a little help from the "arsenal of democracy," as President Roosevelt called it.

Tee listened to the two well-informed men talking about things he knew little about and concluded that if teefin' is a crime it's only a misdemeanor in a world where serious crime ran rampant. He might be a teef but he was just a petty teef.

"They won't be selling any more junk to Germany or Japan," said the Major as he quietly studied the half-filled cup of coffee. They sat in silence for a few minutes and then the Major said, "Tee, you're a young man and that's who fights wars and who gets killed fighting them. You should get back in school while you can. You're clever enough and could do a lot of things besides rewriting the criminal and ethical codes."

There was a look of kindness in the Major's eyes as he continued, "The system doesn't allow people to apply their own unique logic to the rules. We read about Robin Hood and Jesse James and how they became folk heroes. That won't happen to you. When you get caught in the web, there won't be anyone there but you and the spider, and he's the only one who gets to eat. You're on probation, so they're looking at you. Be careful."

"Thank you, Major Manigault. You're right. Mannie keeps telling me the same thing. The problem is that I can't go back to school, I have to work and my daddy, sister, and I have a plan to get our farm back. That takes money, and that's what I'm after. I'll be careful but I can't go back to school," the boy replied earnestly.

Both Mannie and the Major were impressed with what they saw and heard. Tee looked like a boy, but he was a lot more than that. He was a man-child on a mission, and he appeared to be capable of doing what he set out to do. Nonetheless, the men both felt a sense of sadness that they were talking with a young man who had lost his opportunity to be a boy.

Tee broke the silence saying, "Wonder what spider tastes like?"

They laughed and Tee left for the Old Citadel Building to report to his probation officer, leaving the two friends engaged in serious conversation sprinkled with wit and humor.

Chapter 4

On Parole

After the good meal and warm friendship Tee enjoyed at breakfast, the day would only go downhill. He braced himself as he walked the few blocks over to the Old Citadel Building to report to the probation officer. On the ground floor he found the office of Carey Burts and went into a large room with straight-back chairs around the wall and a desk where a kind-faced, middle-aged woman was seated behind an L.C. Smith typewriter. She motioned for the boy to come over and placed a form on the desk.

"What's your name, son?" she asked.

"I'm Tee; Thomas McLauren, Jr., ma'am."

"Sit down, Tee," she replied and motioned for him to pull the chair up to her desk. "We were expecting you yesterday. Did you have some trouble?"

"No, ma'am. They were late getting me released and the train didn't get in until early this morning."

"Where did you spend the night?" she asked with real concern.

"I stayed over at a friend's house. It was too late to wake anyone, and I didn't have a key to my room. I have the key now."

"Your daddy went back to sea; where are you going to live?"

"My sister Mary is at Mrs. Timmons's boardinghouse at 28 Chapel Street and my daddy made arrangements for me to take meals there. He and I have a room on Judith Street. It's all we need. Mary and I will work out something; the rent is paid on the room for six months, so we have that. Mary has a key and she makes sure we don't live in too big a mess. She works at the cigar factory and I will get a job. We know how to get by."

Tee answered all of her questions in a soft, subdued voice. *Look them in the eye and answer their questions in a soft voice*, he was thinking. It was something he learned at Florence. There was lots more.

"Mr. Burts is not in a good mood so be careful when you talk with him. I think you know what I mean," the friendly lady warned Tee. He smiled gratefully at her and replied, "I know." He then walked across the room and knocked gently on the glass-fronted door labeled "Carey Burts."

"Come in," came the gruff reply and Tee opened the door, walked in, and stood before the hostile man's desk, holding his cap in his hands respectfully.

"So, you decided to honor us with your presence. You don't learn, do you? You were due here yesterday and here you show up twenty-four hours late. I suppose you have an excuse," Burts said.

"Yes, sir. The train didn't get in until after one o'clock this morning. I had breakfast and came straight here," Tee answered in the same soft, respectful voice, and with the same passive face.

"Are you going back to school or going to work? You have that choice now. You'd probably do better working, since your daddy left town and you'll probably need the money," Burts said, pulling papers from a file as he spoke. He had turned his chair around and was speaking over his shoulder.

"I think you're right, sir. A job would be best for me at this time," the boy responded with a note of gratitude in his voice. *They like for you to show gratitude* was another thing he learned at Florence.

Burts turned back and faced the boy. He stared fiercely into the passive face before him and after a long period of silence he spoke again.

"You're clever. You act polite and courteous, but you don't fool me. I remember how you struck that man with that chair and hurt him seriously. You and your daddy both. Mean. He did his year and left town. You've done your year and you're back in town. I don't have anything to do with your father, but I have everything to do with you. I have the authority to send you back to Florence and it would please me greatly to do so. You're nothing but trouble, just like your old man, and people like you can't stay out of trouble. You can go now; Mrs. McConnell will give you your schedule on the way out."

The boy bristled inside but practiced his discipline and walked out of the room. Burts had turned his back but Tee could see him watching him from the reflection of a mirror and kept the same passive expression on his face on his way out. He returned to the desk of Mrs. McConnell, who had heard enough of the conversation from the next room to put her firmly on the side of the young man who she regarded as more of a victim than a criminal.

"Are you OK, Tee?" she asked quietly.

"Just another day in paradise," said the boy, using an expression used every day by one of the jailers at Florence.

"That didn't take too long," she added.

"It was longer in there than it was out here," the boy replied with a smile.

"You're bright, son. Be careful. Don't give him anything to use against you," warned the nice lady.

Mrs. McConnell filled out the card for the file and gave Tee his reporting schedule and a copy of the rules of probation. Burts was standing in the door observing the two so they said no more than was necessary to complete their business, but their unspoken communication let Tee know that she was more than a friend: she was also a supporter.

After taking the forms Tee walked down Charlotte Street past the Second Presbyterian Church and turned back down Chapel to have another cup of coffee with Mannie and Major Manigault.

"How did it go?" asked Mannie.

"He really doesn't like me and tried to make me mad so he could pack me back up to Florence. He said that's what he wanted to do. His secretary Mrs. McConnell is a nice lady and warned me against him, not that it was necessary."

Tee ate another ham biscuit and had a cup of coffee before he went to his room on Judith Street.

"I can't stand an overly righteous man," declared the Major as he watched the boy walk up the alley and turn on Chapel Street.

"Me either," said Mannie. "That's probably why you and I are friends. Nobody can accuse us of that."

"Burts probably sees himself lined up with God and on a mission to whip everyone in line. Like the Inquisitor, beat the hell out of the sinners and put them on the road to glory," laughed the Major, looking up from the comfortable position where he lay stretched out on the old sofa. The leather was worn and cracked in spots, but it was still a wonderful place to sprawl. He had poured himself a glass of port wine and he studied his glass and took a good swallow and said, "He would have made a great Inquisitor. Yeah, he would have cheerfully lighted the fire under the heretics. Tee isn't an angel but, besides you and me, there just aren't many of them out there."

They chuckled, gazed again into their glasses and took another sip.

The Major continued, "I don't know of anyone Tee has hurt except those goons over at Jake Burton's, and there he was helping his father. Everyone except the judge knew that Burton had sicced them on Tom and the boy just happened to get there in time to help his daddy bounce a few chairs off their heads. The really bad thing was that Tee got put on probation under Carey Burts, and his daddy got sent to prison."

"Well, that wasn't all bad. Going to prison shocked Tom back to where he gave up drinking and went back to sea. He told me he was going to save his money and try to buy back the farm so that he could get his family back together. Maybe he can…I sure hope so," Mannie said. Then he added, "He started talking to his former shipmates who set things up for him to ship out. He shipped as an able-bodied seaman and said he hoped to get back his bos'n rate."

* * * * *

When Tee left the parole office, Carey Burts sat at his desk thinking about this young delinquent and what it was that gave him an urgent need to bring him under control. On the surface he was calm and controlled yet there was an air about him that was ominous and threatening. Evil. He is evil, was Burts's conclusion and immediately he felt justified and right about his decision to either reform him or send him back to reform school.

When he left his office, Mrs. McConnell was also preparing to leave. He said good evening and left the office with a quick and lively step. He didn't whistle but he felt like it. His bicycle was in the hall and he put a clamp on the right pant leg, rolled the bike out to the street, and pedaled up Rutledge Avenue to his comfortable house and demure little wife. Here he was the lord of the manor. He put the bicycle on the porch of his castle and ended his involvement with the outer world for the day.

Edna Burts worked at the city museum and put in a minimum of eight hours daily leading tours, lecturing, and working with the displays when the public allowed her the time. She loved it and would spend her spare time with her work and her colleagues but never at the expense of her household responsibilities, which were largely centered on Carey and his comfort.

She was sympathetic with him and shared his disappointment when he had had to close his daddy's haberdashery, but they both knew that he didn't have the people skills his daddy had used to build a moderately successful business. The market crash had taken his savings and he found himself struggling along with everyone else to make a living. The appointment to his position as juvenile probation and parole officer was a salvation. They both knew this, but it was never discussed.

The fact that she couldn't have a child never seemed to bother him as it did her, but this subject was something else they didn't discuss. She was educated and academic while he was simply educated. She was deeply devoted to him and was greatly distressed at his accident on the following morning.

He had gotten on his bicycle and headed to work and had turned off Rutledge Avenue to follow his short cut to the office. It was his custom to ride on the sidewalk when he could and as he bumped up from the street the front wheel of his bicycle came off and he crashed. His collarbone was broken, and he spent several weeks at home following his release from the hospital. Everyone around him was puzzled and in their conversations wondered how this could happen to someone as careful as he was about his bicycle. Burts wondered too.

It was painful going back to the office but he walked the same route, stopping to examine the scene of the accident, and with the help of Mrs. McConnell he reviewed the files and paid special attention to Tee McLauren's, but the record showed that he had reported to work as directed. He still wondered, and was convinced that someone had tampered with his bike.

Chapter 5

Taking a Break

Mannie and George Johnson had been talking for a couple of hours when Mannie got up and walked over to his stable, indicating it was break time. The young reporter was surprised because he didn't realize how much time had passed. He found himself fascinated by the man. He was smart, dignified, courteous, and appeared to be seriously interested in telling the story while at the same time protecting the privacy of his friends. There was no question about their friendship. They were friends and from such different worlds. Yes, Mannie was indeed unusual.

The reporter volunteered to help with some chores and was assigned the task of washing the cups and putting on a fresh pot of coffee. He finished and enjoyed watching the chickens scratch and cluck, expressing their pleasure as Mannie sowed the corn. It was fun being there, and he began to see why Major Manigault and Tee McLauren liked it too. It was like a trip to the country, and he began to turn an idea around in his head about a novel he might write. The horse was tended to and things put in order and they sat back down and reopened the conversation.

"This boy, Tee, he had real charm. Everyone liked him," the reporter said.

"No. Not really. He could make you like him, but he didn't turn the charm on people unless he wanted to. He was indifferent to most others and could be tough if he didn't like you. Even for a young man he could be tough," Mannie said. He paused and looked off thoughtfully.

"What do you know of his background?" the reporter asked.

"Things happened in his life that were traumatic," Mannie said. "We're shaped by events and things affect each of us differently. Things had happened that changed his father drastically. Tee was changed, but in a different way from his father and his sister, Mary. She was hurt and saddened but she remained very much as before. We'll talk about all of that later but let me get back to what I was saying."

Chapter 6

Back on the Docks

Tee walked the two blocks to his room on Judith Street, climbed the three flights of stairs and, using the key his daddy had left with Mannie, opened the door and looked around. He smiled. Mary had been there and had cleaned and straightened everything. He knew his daddy hadn't left it that way because his daddy was as poor a housekeeper as he was. No, Mary had been there, and it pleased him. No question about it, men and boys need women around and he sat down a minute and allowed himself to think about his mother and the happy times. Mary was the link to this important memory, and he reminded himself that he shouldn't take it for granted.

But he didn't allow himself to dwell on these thoughts too long. Tee had a discipline that kept him focused on the present and future; the past was too painful, and he wouldn't allow his thoughts to take him there for long. He pulled himself out of his reverie and saw what he was looking for: his bicycle was standing in the corner and his dad had kept it in good shape. He wasn't good at housekeeping, but he was good at maintaining equipment. It was ready for the road.

He gathered up the clothes and other laundry Mary had packed in a bag because she didn't have access to a washing machine. Carrying these things and the bicycle he managed to take it all down in one trip and headed to Mannie's where he ran a couple loads of wash through his machine and hung them out to dry. Mannie was out on his route, so the wagon and horse were gone. The dog and the cat were glad for the company. The dog greeted him warmly with a lot of tail wagging. Tee petted him a while and the dog went back under the shed. The cat had eased down from his comfortable perch on a bale of hay and strode over to where Tee was working and proceeded to rub himself in and around Tee's feet and legs until the boy picked him up and stroked him briefly. After a minute or two of this attention Tee placed the cat back on the ground and watched him stride contentedly back to his perch, where he returned immediately to a state of total rest. From time to time he would open his eyes sleepily and watch… but not for long.

When the clothes were hung out Tee got on the bicycle and headed toward the waterfront, riding skillfully over the old slate sidewalk with its gaps and holes where the slate was broken. He avoided the street where the cobblestones would rattle the bike and the bones of the rider. He knew every break in the sidewalk, having ridden it many times delivering papers and he enjoyed maneuvering the bike around the rough spots and jumping over others; it was a game he had always played and he made good time getting to the railroad property where the sidewalk and the street ended.

Tee entered a field where mountains of junk rose to impressive heights, each looking very much like the other. There were well-worn paths running through the weeds and around the mountains of rusted junk and Tee rode carefully now to protect his tires. He would stop and listen and look for the hobos who built little camps in the junk and under some of the thick brush. He wanted to hide his bicycle and didn't want them to see where he put it because he knew what that would mean. He also knew they were around, but they slept a lot and when he was satisfied that he was not seen he found a spot for the bicycle. It was close to where he used to stake Mannie's horse.

Leaving the junk jungle, the boy proceeded across the main body of railroad tracks to the back lot of an abandoned cotton warehouse where he left the path and made his way through another maze of brush until he found what he was looking for. The bateau was still where he and his father had hidden it under some rusted sheets of metal and then covered it all with tar paper. It looked like a pile of waste.

After checking it over he covered it again and turned back to the path, going directly to the tugboat dock. There he was greeted with a friendly wave and hello from the deckhand who was busy doing what Tee himself would be doing as soon as he made the contact with Captain Henry: scrubbing the decks and swabbing them down, mending ropes and fenders, and in general doing the kind of work that was hard but enjoyable. After working in the muck and mess at Florence, it wouldn't seem like work at all.

As soon as he had spoken with the captain, he joined Leon Sinclair working on the deck and when the cleaning was done, they broke out paint to brighten up the red and black tug with its white stack. Later that day Leon helped him pull the bateau up to the dock where he had obtained permission to tie it up, but not until it had been caulked and painted. It looked good, he thought, and proceeded to fill it with saltwater from the Cooper River and left it to soak and swell the wood before he would try to put it back in the water.

"Good job. Now what you gonna do for oars and locks,

Bubba?" asked Leon, using the common Charleston name for male friends and family.

"I'll find some," answered Tee.

It was getting late when Tee returned to Mannie's to pick up the laundry and found it folded and placed in a box by his old friend. Mannie had lined him up with a Saturday morning job right down from his room on Judith Street.

"You'll like this lady, Tee. She's a widow and her son is a Citadel graduate overseas in Hawaii. She'll be a good friend and needs help around her house from time to time," said Mannie as the boy stacked the box of laundry on the handlebars of the bike and rode off — but not before again expressing his gratitude to his friend.

Chapter 7

Miss Charlotte

Charlotte Smyth Rowland finished her breakfast of oatmeal with coffee and orange juice, checked her schedule of piano pupils for the day, and began to work the daily crossword puzzle in the *News and Courier*. She had settled in her comfortable rocking chair by the window and when she finished the puzzle, she read the rest of the paper. The cat had been slinking around her feet and in and out of her lap announcing that it was time for him to go on his morning prowl, so she let him out onto the porch from where he could wander around to suit himself. The long, wide porch extended along the west side of the house and faced a narrow driveway, which led to a deep backyard as wide as the house and driveway combined. A door opened from the porch to Judith Street, which was the only entrance to the front of the house.

It was Saturday morning and, as was the custom, Miss Charlotte took her broom and swept the steps and the sidewalk. She hummed familiar church music as she swept and when she finished, she waved at her neighbor across the street who was doing the same thing, reentered the door leading onto the porch and went from there into the house.

The arrangement was not unique for a Charleston house; there were many such houses designed to afford privacy in an outdoor setting. She had never lived anywhere else; she was born in this house and it had provided a good home for her to raise her son, William, after the accidental death of her husband. Bill, as she called him, never knew his father, and although he was a good son he was never as close as she wanted him to be. He had access to money when he needed it and even when he simply wanted it. His hobbies occupied his time and his life was centered on these interests, which he pursued very much by himself. There was nothing to complain about; he made good grades in school, never got in trouble, and made her proud when people would praise him to her. She wanted more but didn't nag or conspire to bring him closer to her and accepted the fact that he was mostly a loner.

Bill had graduated from The Citadel two years before and was on active duty in the Army, stationed in Honolulu as a second lieutenant. It was her custom to write him every week because she was able to convince herself that he was homesick, which was not the case. He wasn't a bad son, but he hated to write so she would receive a letter from him no more often than once a month and most often less than that. He hated to write but he loved his mother and didn't want to hurt her feelings, so he forced himself to write very brief letters which were not much more than notes. She saved them all. He also never liked scraping paint off shutters or applying it, so the job would have been open to Tee even if Bill were still at home.

Mannie had told her that he would send a young man around to clean out the gutters and paint the shutters and that he would come today. To make sure that she didn't miss him, Miss Charlotte brought her coffee and lap work out to the porch and placed herself in a comfortable rocker where she sewed and darned while she waited. She didn't wait long because Tee arrived exactly at ten o'clock, as promised.

"Did Mannie tell you what I needed for you to do?" asked the lady.

"Yes, ma'am," replied Tee, being very courteous and standing respectfully before her, holding his cap in his hands in front of him.

"You're not afraid to climb a ladder?" she asked.

"No, ma'am. I'm not afraid to climb. I did a lot of that at school," he said.

"Well, if you look back in the shed, you'll find the ladder, some tools, and the paint and brushes. You might have to look for them, but they're there. The brushes have never been used and some of the paint has not been opened either. Would you like something to eat and drink before you start?" offered the kind little woman. She had taken an immediate interest and liking for such a nice and courteous boy who spoke softly and looked her in the eye as he spoke. She knew he didn't have a mother, a fact which appealed to her sympathy.

"No, ma'am," he said as he left the porch and headed to the shed to look around. Miss Charlotte's ten o'clock student arrived for her piano lesson, so she turned her attention to her pupil and left Tee to his work.

The shed was attached to an open two-car garage and was filled with an accumulation of interesting things, like fishing rods, oars and oar locks, nets, old lumber and a lot of other things, all of which were filed into a mental inventory in the mind of the teef.

Tee put the ladder up against the porch and climbed up to the roof. He was able to remove the leaves from the gutter by hand and, when he finished the porch, he pulled the ladder up and by setting up from the roof of the porch he was able to get on the roof of the house and repeat the process from the upper gutters.

"You be careful up there," warned the small lady, who held her breath as she watched the athletic young man move back and forth across the roof and in particular when he would lean over the edge to remove the leaves. Two hours and a number of warnings later, he came down to start the shutters.

"I've fixed you a sandwich and some tea. Come sit here on the porch and we can have lunch together."

"Thank you, ma'am," said the courteous boy, still using the "school voice."

She studied the young man as he ate and she liked what she saw, a strong boy, large for his age, courteous and hard working. He also smiled a lot when they talked. Tee had made another friend.

Chapter 8

On the Job

Monday morning at eight o'clock Tee stepped onto the deck of the tugboat and spoke briefly with Leon before he started work. First, he scrubbed the deck with a firm-bristled brush with a generous amount of industrial-strength soap. After hosing it down, he mopped it until it was dry, then he went over the side with a chipper and wire brush and began to remove an accumulation of rust and old lead paint. This would take the rest of the day. He took a break for lunch at noon and then went immediately back to the task. Leon took a long break to go down to the marine supply store and when he returned, he tossed a candy bar to Tee and the two of them took a rest break.

"You work too hard," said Leon good-naturedly.

"Well, y'all are nice to give me a job and I appreciate it," replied Tee.

"I hope you don't have your eyes set on my job," said Leon, still smiling at his young friend.

"No, Leon," Tee replied, "I want to own the boat." They both laughed; Leon was amused and failed to see the serious look on the face of his new friend, who was making a visual appraisal of the vessel and thinking it sure would be nice. Leon was a couple of years older than Tee, but he was still a boy and Tee was an adult in a boy's body.

Tee went back to work and stayed at it until five o'clock when he put his tools away and asked Leon if he could put some things in the shed on the dock.

"Sure," said Leon. "Whatta you have you need to lock up?"

"Several things," said Tee and he walked off the dock over to some brush and weeds and returned with a pair of oars, oar locks, a cast net, and a fishing rod and reel.

"Those are nice. Where'd you get them?"

"I've been doing some trading," said the Teef.

The following Saturday morning Tee went straight to Judith Street and finished the painting. Miss Charlotte paid him, and he put his money in his work box and then set about to weed and hoe the long-neglected garden spot between the house and the garage.

When he finished, he put the tools away and started up the driveway to leave when Miss Charlotte spoke.

"Come have some milk and some cake I just made, and how much do I owe you for doing such a fine job in the garden?"

"I think a piece of cake and a glass of milk would be plenty of pay for doing something I enjoyed so much. I'm from the country, you know." He paused and added, "I used to do that all the time for my mother."

He didn't make the statement to arouse sympathy in the kind lady, but it did. After he finished the coconut cake and milk, Tee headed over to Mannie's for a visit and to deliver a generous piece of coconut cake.

About an hour after Tee left Miss Charlotte's house, she had a visit from a man with an arm in a sling who engaged her in serious conversation for half an hour. He had already visited the docks and spoken with Leon.

SUMMER 1939

Chapter 9

The Happy Day

It was mid-afternoon and the tobacco was in the barn. Tom Mc-Lauren was settling up with the hands he had hired to help pull, string, and put the tobacco in the barn and he was ready to fire it up to start the curing process. His wife, July, had gone to the house to plan and fix a good supper for their family of four. Tom, Jr. — everyone called him Little Tee — had unhitched the mules and had taken them to the pasture where they were turned out after a bonus of sweet feed and some corn on the cob. Mary was helping her daddy finish up the business. She was sixteen, a year older than Tee.

Mary worked at any job where she was needed, and she looked pretty, even in overalls and a sunbonnet. She had made her own bonnet, which was sky blue with white trimming, and it framed her healthy, tanned face and showcased her blue eyes. She had worked as hard as anyone but at the present time she was mostly entertaining the group that was assembled under the shed. They liked her and it pleased them to hear her talk and laugh. She had the ability that pretty women often have to amuse and entertain easily and naturally.

No question about it, it was a good day.

The bright leaf was strung on sticks and hung up in the curing barn. The barn had a fireplace at the rear with flues running up and through the barn where the sticks of green tobacco were hung on rafters extending from side to side throughout and from the ground up. The family had all worked to build the barn, using notched logs that they chinked up with clay to make it airtight. They cut their own wood, mixed their own mortar, and put it up piece by piece. The flues were secondhand. Tom bought them at a sale and he and Tee, with a couple of neighbors, had joined them together and hung them in place with metal bands and wires. Tom felt comfortable with the way they were installed but viewed them with concern because they were untested.

Overall, they all felt proud of their efforts and it pleased them, especially Tom, when neighbors and friends complimented their work. In addition to feeling comfortable, he felt proud that in just a few years he had been able to adjust from being a man of the sea to a man of the soil. He agreed to quit the sea when he married July and they moved to the small farm in the Pee Dee she had inherited. Tom made friends easily and learned what their neighbors willingly taught about how to run a small farm. Tobacco was not easy, but it was the money crop. He had a lot of debt, but the crops were thriving, and the tobacco would give him the cash he needed to feel secure. Not totally secure, but comfortable. There weren't many secure farmers. Being a farmer wasn't too different from sailing, he had learned; you were constantly reminded that you weren't in charge and that you were at the mercy of the elements.

The McLaurens' tobacco barn was typical and simple. It had a window at the top front that could be swung open from the outside, primarily to control the heat if the fire got too hot. The wide tin-covered shed extended around three sides of the structure and served as a work and storage area. The tobacco arrived from the fields on a sled, a homemade contraption consisting of a frame of wood built on heavy wooden runners with crocus cloth draped and tacked inside to hold and protect the freshly picked leaves. When the tobacco sleds arrived from the field, the young boys and girls riding the mules would pull the sleds under the shed, get off the mules, and unload the tobacco for the stringers

None of it was easy work but the stringers and handers generally worked in the shade, unlike the croppers, who each took a row and pulled the leaves from the bottom of the plants and put them in the sled. The croppers were mostly men but there were some strong women with sunbonnets on their heads and wearing overalls who could keep up their row. They could also hold their own in the talking, laughing and singing. It was hot, sweaty work being done by hot, sweaty and happy folks.

Stringing was a skill that all tobacco people could do but the best stringers were women, who would usually have one of their children on each side picking up the leaves in hand-sized groups. They handed these to the stringer, who would loop the string around each bundle, then flip the next handful to the other side of the stick. When the stick was completed it had neatly arranged bundles on each side and was handed up into the barn, where it was suspended carefully to allow a free flow of heated air to cure it evenly.

The word "handed" is used a lot in describing the process, but a farmer knew that bright leaf tobacco required more "handing" than any other crop. A bruised or broken leaf was money lost.

Before they started that morning, Tom had promoted Tee from his usual job of pulling the sled to being a cropper. It was symbolic and indicated that the boy was now moving into the role of a man. He called Tee over to the barn where they could talk in private before joining the other croppers who were gathering off to one side with friendly handshakes and jokes.

"I'm moving you out of short pants into long pants," said Tom with his arm over the shoulder of his son. As he spoke, he realized that the fifteen-year-old boy was about as tall as he was.

"I'm not sure that I'm ready. I wouldn't want to mess up by picking some that were too green," replied the boy, his face showing his pleasure.

"You won't mess up but, if you do, you won't be the first or last to pull a leaf or two before it was ready," his father said reassuringly. "You already do a man's work around here; you take care of the animals and can hitch up a mule and plow a good row. You not only milk the cow but know how to take care of her when she needs attention. You're a good hand and you'll be a good farmer," the fond father added.

Tee's protest was not genuine. He knew that he could competently work his row with the adults — better than some — but he knew his daddy would expect some display of modesty. It pleased Tee to have his father express praise for the things he did because praise was not always freely given on this small working farm where everyone had chores and was expected to do them well.

"I'm ready," said the boy and they walked together to join the croppers.

"I've got a new cropper," Tom announced as they approached the others, who all greeted Tee with some handshaking and back-slapping.

"You gonna demand more pay now, I suppose," said Rev. Conyers, who lived with his wife and small daughters on the McLauren farm in a house down by the branch. They were a happy family with little money but plenty of the necessities. "Rev" was his title, which he wore well, whether he was working or preaching at the African Methodist Episcopal Church and he had the respect of everyone around him. Tom and Tee liked to work with him for several reasons. He worked hard and was smart. He knew about animals and plants, but his strong suit was that he knew people. He knew them as a Christian and had the ability to overlook a lot of their Saturday night activity because he appreciated how hard they worked and how hard their lives were. He also didn't forget that he hadn't always been a "man of God." When it got really hot and his back began to hurt from too much leaning and twisting, Rev would either say something amusing or he would sing. It always helped.

Tom answered for his son. "I can't pay him *and* feed him. Rev, if you'll take him home with you, I'll pay him a full wage, but you'll have to feed him."

"Does he eat much?" asked Rev.

"If he went on a diet, I could buy another mule," answered Tom, and the croppers laughed.

"Is he fussy about food?" asked one of the croppers.

"He gets fussy if we run out," said Tom, smiling.

"We never run out at my mama's table," said the proud son.

Mary pulled up riding a mule and pulling a sled and without too much delay they greeted her and bent their backs and began to gather the leaves from the bottom of the stalk. They worked bent over except to put the leaves in the tobacco sled, which gave them a chance to straighten up and walk from their row over to the sled. The sun was hot, and the tobacco left its usual deposit of smelly tar on the skin and hair of the pickers. No one complained about the tar, but it was alright to mention the heat and moan out loud about their sore backs. A loud moan always brought a sympathetic response and a laugh. Tee had joined the club and although he knew he wasn't yet a man, he also knew he was no longer a boy. The row couldn't get too long or the sun too hot for him, and he set out to prove his daddy right.

They had been working steadily for about two hours, mostly in silence with only an occasional moan or comment. Rev and Tom were ahead of the others when Rev stopped and stood in the middle of the row with his hands on his hips and a huge smile on his face. Everyone stopped and straightened out their backs and rubbed the sore or tired places. They also smiled because they knew that Rev was fixing to sing out.

"Go down Moses…….way down to Egypt lan..aa..aand. Tell ole Fay.. aa..ro..oo..oh…" He waited, then joined in with the others when they sang:

"Let my people go."

There wasn't anyone in the area who didn't know the spirituals well enough to join in but the leader was Rev. Conyers. They only sang this brief passage and laughed when they finished.

"You think ol' Tom McLauren gonna let us go?" asked a cropper.

"Not today, we got Rev but he ain't no Moses," said another as they turned back to the work feeling better and not quite as hot or tired. Rev knew when to provide the relief. The day went well and ended as the sun was sinking. They would all sleep well tonight.

It was a good time for the McLauren family. This crop had been a gamble from the start and the pressure had had its effect on Tom, who hadn't been very cheerful or humorous for some months now. Tobacco was the badly needed cash crop and the family was directly impacted by its success or failure.

There was more than the risk of loss involved that had ridden the shoulders of the strong forty-year-old man; the work was constant and demanding and the heat was often brutal out in the field. The heat, the smell of the tobacco plant, the tar from the leaves that would coat the skin with a gummy brown gunk were just part of the hardships. A tobacco crop required constant personal attention. Each leaf had to be watched and protected from worms and bugs. Breaking the flowering tops, pulling suckers from between the leaf and the stalk, picking large ugly worms from the leaves…it went on and on.

In early spring Tom and Tee had set the almost microscopic seed out in a bed of protected and rich soil, then covered the bed with a screen of gauzelike material to keep it shaded from the sun. They checked on it every day. Once they were sufficiently rooted, the young tender plants were set out in the field one by one, making sure they were placed just right on the hill and far enough apart to allow growing room. Tobacco — always called "bacca" in conversations — was a money crop but the man who planted it never quit worrying and working over it until the auctioneer at Lake City or Mullins had knocked it down to a buyer.

Tom thought about these things as he finished his business with his helpers, some of whom worked for wages and some of whom were paying the family back for having helped them get their crop in. They worked reciprocally with each other at this crucial time when the crop had to be pulled and put in the barn for curing. Some things needed to be done at just the right time and farmers either learned this or went out of business, which was what a lot of them were doing during this hard time of depression. Tom knew that surviving required a lot of good luck, but he also had a Presbyterian's view of life and practiced the ethic of working hard and praying too. Tom believed that being Presbyterian was natural for farmers. You worked the crop, but you prayed for rain. It wasn't hard for a man to find his place in this world. When those tender little plants were set out, they needed rain and sun, and not too much of either. A farmer knew where his authority ended and the Supreme took over.

It was a good day. The more difficult the task, the greater the reward and in this case the reward was rich. The look in July's eyes and the smiles they exchanged when she patted his shoulder and headed up the sandy road to fix the meal were pictured in his mind even as he went about his other business. Tom McLauren was smiling again, and it was contagious.

Tee walked back from the pasture to the tobacco barn for no other reason than to share the good feeling and to walk back to the house with the father and sister he loved and admired. After tending to the stock, he had drawn water from the well and filled several tubs that he put out in the sun to heat up for bathing. They could enjoy a good meal, a good bath and a good night's sleep. Tom would light the fire in the curing barn after supper and Tee would take over in the morning. Everyone slept in shifts.

Curing bright leaf was a twenty-four-hour business that required a constant temperature. The furnace was long and oval. It was built to accommodate long but small logs, which were moved into the fire as the demand for heat increased and would be pulled back out to lower the heat when necessary. If the heat got too high you could open the door, the window, or both to cool it down.

The county's road scraper had come by as they were finishing up and the big blade had turned the rutted sand into a smooth surface. The freshly turned sand was cool to their feet. The three of them had taken off their shoes, tied the laces together and slung them over their shoulders and were playing like children, pushing and hugging on each other. Some pleasures are so simple that they can best be realized through looks, glances and touches. It had been a long time since the children had seen Tom in a relaxed mood. It was truly a good day and they would never forget it.

After more jostling around the washbasins on the back porch

and helping July put the dinner on the table, they bowed for Tom's prayer.

"Lord…You know how grateful we are for your goodness to this family. You have given us work to do and the ability to do it. We've worked hard to put our crop in the ground, and you have blessed us with good weather to make it grow. We thank you for what's in the barn and for what's in the field but, most of all, we thank you for the love and happiness you have allowed us to have. Bless this family and this meal and accept our humble thanks. Amen."

Tee went straight off to bed after supper and a good bath. Tomorrow he would take his turn tending the barn. Mary would do the same after helping her mother put the dishes away and they would both go to their beds happy for having had this great day.

Chapter 10

Firing the Barn

Tom took the truck with a load of logs to the curing barn and, after starting the fire with pine knots, he began to feed the small fire with more logs and kindling. It soon responded and the heat immediately commenced to circulate through the flues and around the suspended sticks of strung tobacco. He opened the door and realized that the thermometer was in the horse barn and he would have to get it, but he also knew that July would come pretty soon to bring him some coffee and something to feed on during the night and he could get the thermometer then.

In the meantime, he would keep the fire at a moderate heat. You didn't want to put too much heat on the leaves at first. After a couple days of moderate heat, the temperature was raised substantially to cure the stems. It was another hands-on process but a lot more pleasant than putting the leaves in the barn. Tomorrow night the family would all come down for a while and they would churn ice cream and roast peanuts and other things they enjoyed. It was more of a party than a chore but curing tobacco was a serious business with serious consequences if it wasn't done right. Tom McLauren would do it right. No one doubted that.

It hadn't been dark long before he could see the figure of his wife silhouetted against the white sandy road. There was a good moon, so she didn't carry a lantern. She was barefooted and smiled happily when she came under the shed with the coffee and food for Tom.

"Watch the barn for me for a few minutes. I left the thermometer in the horse barn where I was cleaning it off. It won't take long."

"Sure. Do you want me to do anything while you're gone?"

"No. Just watch. And don't eat my cake."

"How did you know it was cake?"

"I know you. You always bring me cake, and I always love it… just like I love you," answered Tom over his shoulder as he got into the stripped-down Chevrolet truck and drove off, chuckling.

July looked around and began to arrange things. She wasn't that neat or orderly, she just had to be busy and had trouble just sitting around. The fire was burning faster now, and she opened the door to keep it from getting too hot inside while she waited. She stopped and turned as she heard an unusual sound from the rafters. After looking up and around the hanging tobacco she went back to picking up and arranging things. She heard the sound again but dismissed it as coming from the heat being released into the barn and the change in temperature in the flues.

Meanwhile, Tom had reached the barn and found the thermometer. He was looking around to see if there was anything else he needed when he heard the sound from outside. He listened intently and wasn't sure whether he heard something or what it was that caught his attention. When he heard it again, he knew.

GOD! GOOD GOD!! IT'S THE BARN. He stumbled and fell as he ran for the truck. He couldn't find the keys, so he ran toward the barn panicking and yelling. He could see the flame leaping out the door. Reaching the barn, he circled it, calling for July, then ran inside the flames and pulled her from under the fallen sticks of tobacco. His hair and clothes were on fire when his neighbor Joe Freeman arrived and covered him with a cotton sheet and wrestled him to the ground. Other neighbors who were tending their barns had seen the flame and came rushing to help. When they arrived, July was still and not breathing. Tom was hysterical and several friends held him down while they sent for help.

"Get Tee!" someone yelled.

"Leave the children alone. They can't help and they'll know soon enough," replied Joe.

Friends were able to calm Tom down enough so that he could gather July in his arms, and he held on to her and stroked her scorched hair while his friends applied Vaseline to his head and arms, which were severely burned. Others turned away and stood looking off, consumed in their own sadness and grief. There were no dry eyes. The happy day was over.

Chapter 11

Selling the Farm

The next day Tom was up early and doing the routine chores. When he got to the horse barn, he saw Tee and Rev, who had already fed the mules. Tee was milking the cow while Rev was checking to see if there was enough water in the trough and putting other equipment away. They went about their work in silence, neither wanting to trespass on the grief of the other. When he finished his work, Tom took Rev off to one side and they had a brief conversation after which they shook hands solemnly and Tom cranked up the truck.

"Where you going?" asked Tee, as he walked over to the truck and put his foot on the running board.

"Into town. We've got to see what we can do. I thought I'd go to the bank and see what they wanted me to do," replied Tom, his red-rimmed eyes looking toward the tobacco barn, which was still smoldering.

"I'll go with you. Let me tell Mary. I'll be right back," Tee said over his shoulder as he turned toward the house.

When Tee came back, he had hurriedly changed clothes and with his serious countenance looked much older than fifteen. He was; he had aged several years in just forty-eight hours.

They rode in silence for a few miles, then Tom said, "The bank will let me know where I stand, and I can start making decisions about what we can sell and where we can go from here."

"Maybe we should talk to Cousin Henry first. We ought to have a plan before we go to the bank," Tee said, looking at his father. Tom seemed to be operating in a cloud of uncertainty and doubt. "Henry will probably be more help to us. The bank will be more interested in collecting their money than in helping us get a good sale," Tee continued, as his father turned to look at him for the first time since they started the trip. Tom studied the face of this young man who had suddenly taken on a more mature role.

It was thirty minutes later that they stopped in front of the bank. Tom walked to the door and read the posted schedule of banking hours and saw that it was not due to open for another hour.

"Let's go to Henry's office. We don't want to meet up with a lot of people who mean well but who will want to talk about things we don't want to talk about right now," Tee said, and again Tom turned to look at his young son who was offering such good advice.

They walked around the square without getting close enough to anyone to require conversation and ended up at the law office of Tom's cousin. They climbed a flight of stairs to a dimly lit hall and came to a glass-paneled door labeled "Henry McLauren, Attorney." The office was plain but adequate for a small-time lawyer in a small-time town. It was too early for anyone to be at work, but there was a comfortable old sofa in the hall where the dazed and weary man sat and stared blankly at the wall and then the ceiling, thankful for the privacy and quiet.

Tee strolled around the hall briefly, then went down the stairs and came back a few minutes later with two paper cups of black coffee. Tom wasn't sleeping but was surprised when he felt the hand on his shoulder and heard Tee offering him the coffee, which he accepted with something akin to pleasure. It was strong and it was black, and it had a good effect on the tired man. Tee went back down the stairs, leaving Tom alone with his thoughts. They didn't want to talk about what had happened and they couldn't think of anything else to talk about.

Things had changed. The strong-willed Tom was struggling to regain control of his thoughts and life. Tee had gone to bed two nights before a country boy contented with his simple life of doing his chores and enjoying his family. This morning he stood in the doorway of the law office consumed with thoughts of how to gather their assets and make the best sale possible.

It was early for Henry, but someone who had seen Tom go in the office called to let him know that Tom was waiting. He soon arrived. "Y'all come on in," he said, unlocking the door.

Henry had planned to go to the farm later that day to see the family and to offer help. Driving into town, he reflected on the sketchy information he had heard and had a good idea of what the problems were and what he needed to do. Tom's precarious financial situation was not a secret. Henry had helped make the financial arrangements with the bank and was familiar with when the notes were due and the consequences for failure to pay on time. He had helped get extensions for Tom as well as most of the other farmers who were struggling to keep their land and he also knew that the tobacco crop was their hope for generating enough cash to keep afloat. Everyone knew that Tom was finished as soon as they heard the news about the barn fire.

"I guess I'll have to sell as soon as possible," Tom said. "My crops are valuable and can be sold standing in the field. My tobacco has to be sold immediately. My barn is gone so I have no place to cure it. There are several farmers around who can make room in their barns and who might be interested in picking it up."

"Maybe you could get one of them to allow you to use their barn," Henry suggested.

"No. It wouldn't be fair to put someone on the spot like that," Tom said. "Even if they have room, it would be too much inconvenience to ask them to reschedule everything to accommodate me. I'm through, Henry. Even if I had access to a barn, I don't have the strength or will to continue. Without July, I'm finished. What I have to do now is gather as much money as I can and make plans for my family."

"What do they want to do?" asked Henry.

Tom shook his head. "I don't know. Mary will be a senior in high school this year and she will probably want to finish with her friends. She and Tee should be together. They'll complain and want to come with me but that wouldn't be good. No. I'll pay someone to keep them in their home this school year," Tom said, almost to himself.

"Sue and I want to keep them with us. We talked about it last night. We have plenty of room and they like us and know how much we like them," Henry said, looking at his cousin earnestly as he spoke. Tom knew that he meant it.

"Thank you, Henry. You and Sue are true friends."

Tee sat quietly next to his father and listened without comment. He thought it was good of Henry and Sue to offer to take them in, but he knew what he was going to do. It was a good plan for Mary, but he knew full well that he was going wherever his father went and no one would change that.

"I need to go to the bank and see where I stand there," said Tom. "It doesn't make sense to plan ahead until we know how long a rope we're tied to."

"Let me do it," Henry said. "I have all your records and I know your financial situation as well as I do my own. Time is what we need and that has to be bargained for. Dempsey is a good fellow but it's to his advantage to move quickly to keep the account off his debt list. The regulators write them up for delinquent accounts and we've been on the list for some time. It's not a short list and I can bargain for you better than you can for yourself, especially now. Leave it to me and you go talk to Mary and Tee about their plans. We need to find a buyer for the farm. We can sell the crops independently if the bank will release them from their lien, but I'd rather find someone to buy it all. I know some prospects. Go home and I'll get in touch with you later. Go see Rev. McLeod, who has already called me about funeral arrangements. You don't need to worry about the bank right now; let me do that."

Tee was moved by the generosity of his father's cousin and studied the two men, who sat quietly for a few minutes. They'd always been close and felt comfortable together. After a while, Henry turned to Tee and said, "You'll like it with us, Tee, and we will like having you too."

"Thank you, Cousin Henry," said Tee. "You're generous and we thank you for your help." He spoke sincerely but gave no indication of his personal plans.

Tom looked earnestly into the eyes of his cousin, shook his hand, and left.

* * * * *

Mary had been busy cleaning and cooking and when she saw the truck pull into the yard and park under the pecan tree. She called her father and brother to breakfast. They usually parked the truck under the pecan tree when they planned to use it again right away, otherwise it was put in the barn. She studied their faces as they walked toward her.

"Have you eaten yet?" Mary asked.

"I'm not hungry. I'll have something later," replied Tom. After a moment he said, "Henry is talking to the bank for us. You know what we have to do. We have to sell as quickly as possible so we can get a good price for our crops and we need to make plans for next year. I'm going over to the church to meet with Rev. McLeod and then to the mortuary to make arrangements. Sue is already there, selecting the things we'll need," Tom said, choosing to refer to the casket and shroud as "things." "Rev. McLeod will plan the service. I just have to approve the things they set up."

Tom was looking at the ground as he spoke, and the two children continued to study his face. They were doing their best. Mary couldn't control her tears, which streaked her face, and Tom was pale and red-eyed. Tee's face was pale, but he wasn't crying.

"What can we do to help you, Daddy?" asked Tee.

"Just keep things together here. There'll be a lot of people coming and someone will need to receive them," Tom suggested softly. "I guess we need to dress up a little. Mary, you do what you can in the house, and Tee, you take care of everything else and help her if you can."

Chapter 12

Leaving it Behind

The John Calvin Presbyterian Church sat on a little knoll. It was built originally around 1800 by the Scotch Presbyterians who settled the area and developed well-tended acres of sandy but productive land. They built the school and the church. The cypress lumber was cut, hauled out of the swamp, sawed, and fashioned into the neat but small church with a modest steeple and hard pews. The school was even plainer.

They mostly held farms ranging from one hundred to several hundred acres and had traditionally planted and harvested their own crops. There was little social activity among them except for the church and the school, both of which they took great interest in, and their work, of course. They would help each other put their crops in the barn. They also exchanged information about farming in general, but this was done mostly when they gathered in the churchyard where they hitched their horses.

The McLauren family sat together at the front of the church while Rev. McLeod conducted the service. All of the pews were full, and many people were standing around the walls. They sang traditional hymns that most of them knew by heart and Tom seemed to be comforted by the music and the service. Tee held Mary's hand and sat in silence. He could see the cemetery through the old windows that distorted the headstones with their wavering imperfections. His eyes came to rest on the green tent standing over the freshly opened grave with the artificial grass carpet and folding chairs placed in readiness for the last ritual. He comforted his sister but never shed a tear during the service. His mind was more set on the problems his father was facing than it was on the ceremony.

When the short graveside service was completed, the people wandered out from the graveyard and stood talking in small groups. They all repeated their condolences to the family and left; some of them visited family gravesites before leaving. Tee said little but accepted the family's friends graciously with thanks and handshakes. It finally ended and the McLaurens went home to take inventory of the things they expected to keep and sort them out from the things that were expendable. Rev and his family had been at the service and followed them to the house where they pitched in and helped with the remaining chores.

Several days passed before Cousin Henry appeared with the word from the bank. He had done a good job of pitching his plan, which allowed Tom to sell the crops in the field and deed the farm to the bank. This could be done by placing a clause in the deed excepting the existing crops from the conveyance. Henry had also gotten a reasonably good price for the crops, stock, and equipment. They kept the truck. The bank agreed to allow Rev and his family to stay on, which was as much to their advantage as it was to the family's. Tom also gave his friend a mule and a calf that were not in the bank's inventory.

It was about seventy miles from the farm to Charleston, but the Chevy truck held up well and, even with a fair load, they had an uneventful trip. Never driving over forty miles an hour, they made the trip in a couple of hours and arrived at Judith Street, where Henry had arranged for a one-room apartment for the men. Tee had made it clear to everyone that he was staying with his father. They were able to persuade Mary to return on the train and finish her senior year while living with her cousins. It took a lot of persuasion to make her accept the plan, but she relented finally with the comforting knowledge that when school was out, she would be a Charlestonian too.

They made the necessary contact with the landlord and proceeded to unload the truck and haul the furniture up three flights of stairs to their modest room. Mary, even dressed in overalls, attracted the attention of several young men who volunteered to help. She didn't need to try to be attractive, it was natural, and, in this instance, it was very helpful. What would have been a difficult chore was handled quickly by the five men and one strong girl with pretty hair, blue eyes and a smile that young men couldn't resist.

Adversity has to be faced, and work is good medicine for sorrow. With so much activity taking place in such a short time, the family didn't have time to dwell on their losses. They had lost the things they treasured the most — the farm, their style of living, and, above all, the anchor of their lives. Tom and Mary would show their sorrow through their eyes. Tee never showed anything except quiet resolve and determination. Work was necessary, but it was also good.

Tom forced some payment on the helpful young men, who took the money reluctantly. They took turns trying to impress Mary, who was gracious and smiling but anxious to get to the room and arrange the house for the only men in her life. To help her make the break, Tee handed her a basket of fragile things and she mounted the steps cautiously while she declined the offers to help put forth by the attentive young men. Once in the building and on the stairs, she took the steps two at a time and closed the door behind her when she reached the room.

A little later she looked around the well-arranged one-room apartment and took a seat in her mother's rocker and relaxed. The next morning, she was on the Coast Line train headed back to finish her last year of school. Tee wandered off, studying the area, and Tom went to the docks, where he had some old friends and found a job checking and tallying freight being unloaded from a ship. Another page was turned, and new challenges were being faced.

Chapter 13

A New Home

The first day had gone well and the reporter was in high spirits when he returned the next day and picked up the interview. "How did Tee get in trouble?" asked the reporter. He had moved over to Major Frank Manigault's old cracked leather chair and was laid back much as Mannie's old friend had been so many times in the past.

Mannie stared at the young man briefly before he answered. "The trouble started with his daddy. His daddy couldn't cope with the loss of his wife. He tried hard but he couldn't focus on the things he needed to do. Drinking. That's what men do when they get lost and that's what he did. He found work on the docks but started hanging out at Jake Burton's joint on Calhoun Street and you don't have to look any further to find serious trouble…It was on a Saturday evening in the early winter of 1940 when Tee got involved."

Mannie began the story, the reporter leaning forward eagerly.

"Tee had spent the night in my barn, something he had started doing from time to time. When he got home, a neighbor told him his daddy hadn't come home the night before, and that he'd been drinking again."

Tee thanked his neighbor and set out to walk the four blocks from Judith Street to Jake Burton's. Jake's was a seedy beer joint with a broken neon sign flashing the letters JA E'S. It was getting dark and the drinking crowd was moving about when he arrived to see a crowd overflowing into the street. He pushed his way inside and saw the source of the excitement.

"Tom McLauren was backed into a corner holding a chair and punching it toward two big and unruly men armed with bottles who were cursing and threatening him. Tee didn't hesitate. He picked up a chair and struck the biggest one behind the head and turned to the other, who raised the bottle to strike the boy. Tom struck him on the head with a chair before he could crash the bottle on Tee's head. Tee took a position beside his father, both still armed with chairs, now broken. Jake Burton came out from behind the bar and was cursing and yelling when the police arrived.

"Arrest that man," yelled Burton, pointing to Tom. "He owes me fifteen dollars and has been causing trouble all day long."

Mannie continued, "Tom said he didn't owe Jake anything, and then said he had sicced his goons on him to steal his money. Jake wasn't having any of it. 'Lock em up. Both of them. I'll press charges for destroying my property. He causes trouble every time he comes in and they both broke my chairs over my waiters. I want them locked up,' Jake shouted.

"That's how Tee's troubles started," Mannie said. "They took them to jail and Tom was held because he couldn't make bail. They turned Tee over to the juvenile court and he was put on probation. That's where he fell under the control of Carey Burts. It was three months before Tom was sentenced to one year in prison. They gave him credit for the three months he was held before trial."

"How did Tee end up in Florence?" the reporter asked.

"Burts found out that Tee was selling junk to different dealers around town and figured out where he was getting it. It was from the railroad yard, of course. Burts alerted the railroad detectives and they caught Tee. They revoked his probation and he had to serve the year at Florence."

"So that's where he was when his daddy got out of prison and went back to sea," observed the reporter.

"Yeah, Tom still had some contacts and had kept his papers in order. He was also embarrassed about going to prison. The fact is that Tee's mama was the cement that held them together. When she died it broke the bond. Mary and Tee grew up real fast. Tee turned into a man and they both took responsibility for their father. Tom tried but he'd lost his manhood. That's probably why he went back to sea. He knew he had to find it again and that it wasn't in a bottle down on Calhoun Street."

"So, Tee was sent up a few months before his father was getting out?" asked the reporter.

"Yes, and that's when Mary came back. As soon as she heard about Tee and Tom, she dropped out of school and came here. Their cousins tried to get her to stay but she was determined and caught a bus to Charleston. She shared a room at Mrs. Timmons's boardinghouse and got a job at the cigar factory."

"That's pretty rough work," said the reporter.

"Well, Mary was pretty, but she was also strong. Working with tobacco at the factory wasn't harder than working it in the field or the barn. Tobacco is a smelly weed and it requires plenty of hand work at every stage, but she was more than capable. A woman can be both pretty and tough and she was both. The only other job available was at Kress's dime store, and they had a long list of young girls looking for work and they didn't pay near as much as at the factory."

"How did she get along with the other girls at the factory and the boardinghouse?" asked the reporter.

"I guess it's natural for people to resent others prettier than they are but that passes if the person is also nice and friendly. They not only liked her, but competed for her friendship, especially after the incident with The Citadel cadet."

"What was that about?" asked the reporter, curiosity further roused.

Mannie had been stirring around as they talked, sharpening a kitchen knife. Now he took a seat on the leather sofa, put down the knife and continued his tale.

SPRING 1941

Chapter 14

Mary at Work

The girls at the cigar factory on Columbus Street worked in smocks and they tied their hair up in kerchiefs. The tobacco was placed on worktables and they would select the filler and begin to shape a roll and proceed until they completed the cigar by tightly rolling it into a wrapper leaf. Tobacco leaves a stain and a smell on and about anyone working with it but it's a part of the process and you get used to it.

Mary had gotten the job through Essie, one of the girls at Mrs. Timmons's boardinghouse, and they worked at adjoining tables. Essie was a stout country woman with a good face and disposition. It was easy for Mary to become her friend, and on the weekends, they would purchase supplies and do each other's hair. The girls at the boardinghouse all practiced hairdos on each other, the favorite being the perm kit. It not only smelled bad — far worse than the tobacco — but the finished product was a tangle of tight curls impossible to comb. They would laugh at each other and try something else to change the texture or color of their hair the next weekend.

Some of the girls had boyfriends but Mrs. Timmons screened them so closely that most of them spent their leisure time working on their wardrobes and learning the words to the latest song on the radio: "A tisket, a-tasket, a green and yellow basket" and "The music goes around and around." They also taught each other dances like the Big Apple and the Charleston. They had fun together and mostly saved their money or sent it back to their families in the country. Mary saved.

At the factory they worked hard. The bosses kept the place hot and humid, which took its toll on the energy and patience of the workers. Quarrels and even fights would sometimes break out between some of the more physical girls and they always left Mary with a sick feeling inside. She got along with all of her co-workers by just being herself and being pleasant to everyone.

Once a year, The Citadel, the military college in Charleston, assigned its cadets to do time-motion studies at the factory. They set up their clocks and cameras at workstations and critiqued the efforts of the workers. The girls didn't like it. They didn't trust the cadets, who they saw as being in cahoots with the bosses to get more work out of them for less pay. They also perceived the cadets as rich college boys from a different planet. Neither of these were true.

First, the boys were taking a course in business economics and the time-motion studies were merely a class assignment. The cigar factory bosses might make use of their findings but that was unlikely. Their finished product was not of a highly professional quality and was of more interest to the professor and the students than anyone else.

The cadets didn't enjoy the task much either. They weren't from another planet, but they were stunned by the atmosphere of the factory. The oppressive heat and tobacco smell hit as soon as they entered, and the girls weren't shy about expressing their opinions of the neatly dressed intruders. Very uncomplimentary comments were tossed back and forth between some of the more aggressive workers, which either angered or intimidated the cadets. Most learned to tune the workers out while they went about their business. They couldn't wait to get out of the factory as soon as they could and put the day behind them…with one exception.

Charlie Rowland's eyes had fallen on the girl of his dreams. He had his camera set on Essie, but his eyes were on Mary. It was a Cinderella dream in which he saw her smock as a formal gown. Soon he was mentally scripting romantic roles for himself and the beauty queen he had discovered in such an unlikely place.

When the bell rang to end the day, he waited around on the Columbus Street side of the factory and as Mary and Essie came out, he politely approached them and offered to escort them home. All efforts to discourage him failed and he walked to the gate at 28 Chapel Street, where the boardinghouse was, and where they were able to leave him on the sidewalk. They weren't rude, but they were discouraging.

Once they were inside, Essie chastised Mary for not being more encouraging to such a good-looking and obviously nice young man.

"They don't grow on trees, you know," she said.

"I know, Essie," Mary said, "but I don't have room in my life for anything else and I don't want to lead him on. He is nice, and he is good-looking, but I am not interested."

The next day when the bell rang, Charlie was waiting and walked them home again. Mary would not allow him to engage her in conversation, but Essie was courteous and the two of them talked until they again came to the gate of the former mansion house where they lived. There Mary said, "Please don't keep this up. I know you are a nice young man and only mean to be friendly, but I'm not available. I have too many things to do as it is, and I don't have room for your friendship. If you wait for me again, I will have to report you to your professor, who I know would not approve of one of his students forcing his attention on a worker at the factory."

Charlie's face turned red. "I'm sorry," he said. "It won't happen again."

The girls watched as he turned and walked to the bus stop on Alexander Street and got on the beltline trolley. Essie chastised Mary again, but stopped when she realized Mary didn't want to hear any more. Mary went into the kitchen and sat on a stool talking with Mrs. Timmons. They talked about cooking and recipes for a while, but then Mary got up and went to her room.

She wasn't happy.

Chapter 15

Back at Jake Burton's

Saturdays were always big days for Jake. They started as soon as he opened at ten o'clock in the morning and got busier as the day went on. He closed the doors at midnight, but the action continued in the back room until early Sunday morning. Tip boards and other gambling devices generated a lot of cash, while the pool tables in the back kept the crowd occupied. The serious players drank little, but the spectators kept emptying the beer cooler. In the nine-ball games the bets got bigger as the night wore on and, of course, Jake pinched the pot after each rack.

Sandwiches and snacks went along with the pool shooting and beer drinking and it kept employees jumping, including the two goon waiters who had provoked the fight with Tom McLauren in 1940 that had resulted in him going to prison and Tee falling into the clutches of Carey Burts.

Everything had gone downhill quickly for the McLaurens after that. After he was released from prison, Tom had gone back to sea and no one knew what was happening with him. Mary had quit school and come to Charleston to be of whatever help she could to her family. Tee had been sent to the reform school in Florence. Jake's was the source of a lot of expense and misery for the McLaurens.

The bar up front faced Calhoun Street with the poolroom located to the rear. It was a converted warehouse building, a deep one, with thick walls. Behind the poolroom was Jake's sanctuary, where he retired after work and counted his money. The thick walls made the room almost soundproof and it was an ideal retreat from the noise and smoke of the bar.

The space was comfortably furnished with heavy old furniture and modern appliances, but the greatest joy for Jake was the deep and wide bathtub with its efficient water heater. He loved to count his money and retire to his hot bath, where he could sip some good whiskey and reflect on his good fortune. His routine was to close the poolroom and send everyone to the bar up front where the goons would continue to serve until about three o'cock when they closed up for the night. The goons would hang out in the kitchen fixing sandwiches for themselves and, after eating, lock up and go home.

On this particular Saturday, it was after one o'clock when Jake emptied the poolroom and locked himself in his sanctuary to count his money. He smiled. It was an exceptional day. He put his money bag in his desk drawer, selected his nightshirt, and went into the bathroom for a long soak while he reflected on the day's profits. He failed to notice the black-clad silhouette of the young man, concealed by the shadows in the corner.

While Jake was luxuriating in the warm water, the shadow moved quietly across the room and removed the money bag from the desk drawer. Then it disappeared through the skylight, which had also provided an entrance. Jake finished his bath and slept happily until noon on Sunday.

It was around two o'clock on Sunday afternoon when the police came into the bar, where they were met with an irate man with two subdued and severely chastised employees. Jake gravitated between charging the two with outright theft of his money and with being so negligent as to allow someone to enter the back room and take it. Even while he was accusing them, he knew that neither charge was likely; he had the only key to the back room. However, this knowledge did nothing to moderate his rage, which he continued to direct at the two goons, now simply pathetic employees.

The officer called for backup and a detective arrived who immediately set about looking for other possibilities. He went through the building first, and then he walked outside and searched for an entry from either a window or the roof. It took some time before he could get a ladder tall enough to examine the roof, but when it came, he found his answer.

"Someone scaled the drainpipe and came in through the skylight on the roof," the detective advised Jake. "Whoever it was had to be strong and athletic to get up there and he most likely used a rope to come down into the room and to leave."

"I still don't see how that was possible," sputtered the angry bar owner.

"It's not possible for you or me, that's why I said it had to be someone who was athletic and strong," the detective said positively, indicating he had no doubt in his mind. "Very few people could pull it off."

The goons were much relieved but kept out of sight anyway. They knew that no apologies would be made but they also knew that the heat was off them.

That same day, Tee joined Mary at Mrs. Timmons's for the noonday meal and enjoyed the good food and conversation among pleasant people. He didn't say much but he seemed to smile more than usual.

On Monday, Carey Burts read in the *News and Courier* about the incident at Jake Burton's and wondered about Thomas Mc-Lauren, Jr. So did Mannie Simmons and Major Frank Manigault.

Chapter 16

Summertime and the Living Is Easy

The lines from *Porgy and Bess* about summertime always came to mind for Miss Charlotte, who loved flowers and other growing things, when it came time to start her summer garden. Her small garden plot was a source of real pleasure when she could put on her bonnet, get out her hand tools, and dig and plant.

It was a pretty Saturday morning and she greeted it eagerly by rising early and launching into her chores with new energy. Spring always did that for her. She was reborn along with all the outdoor things that made her happy: birds, squirrels, trees and everything else that came to life at this time of year. She was especially eager to welcome Tee and Mary, who were coming to get the plot ready for planting. Tee had introduced his sister to the gracious lady, whose motherly instincts were aroused by the motherless young woman, just as they had been with Tee. She hadn't told Mary about someone else who was coming but who would not arrive until after the Saturday morning parade at The Citadel.

Mary arrived first and started working in the kitchen while Miss Charlotte swept the steps and sidewalk out front. Mary sensed that the little lady was engaged in the practice of a ritual rather than a chore, so she put on the kettle to make tea and set to dusting and cleaning things that were too high for her petite hostess to reach.

Tee arrived shortly and went directly to the garage to get the plow and hand tools. He brought them to the plot and went inside to visit with the two women whose company he enjoyed so much. He had enjoyed Mary's company all his life, and he enjoyed Miss Charlotte's company more with each meeting. Sandwiches and iced tea were musts for these small gatherings, along with the happy chatter between the ladies. Tee liked to look and listen, and his commentary came in the form of smiles more often than words.

"How do you like your work?" Miss Charlotte asked Mary.

"Most of the time it's OK but sometimes it gets boisterous and loud," Mary replied, thoughtfully choosing her words. "Some of the girls don't get along well and they aren't shy about how they express themselves. They say a lot of things that you'd rather not have to listen to, but that's not what bothers me the most. I hate violence and sometimes they come too close to physically fighting. They're all nice to me and I think it's the pressure of the heat, and some of the bosses bear down pretty hard on the slow ones." She concluded, "I'm it for the money and never expected it to be any different when Essie got me the job."

"How about you, Tee?" asked the lady.

"I'm fine, Miss Charlotte," he said. "I like my job and the people I work with. I get to fish from the dock and sometimes I go out on the boat. Leon shows me where to fish and when. I'm doing very well."

"What do you catch?" she asked.

"From the dock, mostly croakers," Tee said. "Leon went

with me to Castle Pinckney and we caught some sheepshead. He showed me now to use steel leaders because they bite through a regular rigging. He said we could catch some drum under the bridge, but we haven't tried that yet. Leon likes to fish with a hand line, and I think he'll have a hard time pulling in a drum by hand. He says he does it a lot and I believe him. He's strong."

"You're strong too, Tee," said Mary. "I couldn't believe how much you'd grown when I first saw you after you came back from Florence."

"Good food and gentle care," replied Tee, and they all laughed.

It was close to eleven o'clock before Tee pulled his chair back and headed to the garden. Mary sat a little longer before she too broke off the chitchat and followed her brother. They were both dressed like field hands and felt good about getting into the soil again. Miss Charlotte soon joined them in an old full dress and a bonnet. They exchanged looks and grinned, then threw themselves into the task of chopping and tilling the good black earth, some of which was hard, especially the new part Tee was breaking up to enlarge the plot. The push plow would hang up on the hardest parts, so Tee tied a rope to the front and pulled while Mary pushed and guided.

"You make a good mule!" Mary teased.

"Quit riding on the plow, even a good mule needs help," retorted her brother.

"The two of you make a good team," Miss Charlotte said. The three tugged and pulled for more than an hour before she decided a lunch break was in order. They brushed themselves off, washed their hands, and Tee went to the porch to lounge on the comfortable old wicker furniture. Mary went into the kitchen with Miss Charlotte and they fixed more sandwiches and iced tea.

These were rapidly consumed, along with slices of coconut cake.

It was a little after one o'clock when the street door opened and a Citadel cadet in full uniform entered. Miss Charlotte introduced her young cousin. Tee extended his hand to the tall, good-looking young man with the great smile. Mary did likewise, but they had already met. An awkward moment ensued with Mary trying unsuccessfully to conceal her discomfort. Tee and Miss Charlotte were puzzled by her reaction, Tee more than their hostess. Mary was always confident and gracious and accustomed to a lot of attention from young men, even when it was not altogether welcome. Charlie Rowland's smile was soon replaced with a noticeable blush and he too stood awkwardly until Miss Charlotte explained that Charlie was her favorite cousin's son and very popular within the family. She asked him to come to the kitchen with her so she could fix him some dessert and the two left Mary and Tee on the porch.

"What happened to you, Mary?" Tee asked.

"I'm sorry," said Mary. "I'm embarrassed and I can't say why. I met him at the factory, and he walked me home several times until I asked him to stop."

"Why?" asked her brother.

"You know why. The same reason you don't hang out and party with your pals. We're committed to the same thing and we don't have room in our lives for anything else," she said, looking him squarely in the face. She was obviously over the surprise and back in control.

When their hostess and Charlie came back from the kitchen, Mary was gracious and smiling and everyone was soon at ease. Charlie ate his cake with pleasure, went inside, and returned wearing work clothes.

"Lead me to it!" he said with enthusiasm. "I can pull, push, or dig and I'm used to being told what to do."

"You can take my place because I promised Essie I would go downtown with her today," Mary said. "It's good to see you, Charlie. I know you and Tee will do better without me. Two mules are better than one," she teased with a broad smile that left every-one feeling better, especially Charlie.

The young men went to work, and Miss Charlotte retired to the porch and sat in her rocker. Then she smiled, thinking, "in the springtime a young man's thoughts…"

Tee and Charlie waded into the challenge of subduing the hard-packed yard and making it ready for the gentle lady with her small hands. Their age difference never became an obstacle as the two youths demonstrated their strength and commitment to the project. It was a competition of sorts, but in a spirited and friendly way. The fact that Charlie was older and a senior in college didn't intimidate Tee, who didn't have a high school diploma. He was a graduate of "the finishing school for boys" in Florence and even though he was still a boy in years, he was strong and athletic.

Chapter 17

Reporting In

On Wednesday Tee took his lunch hour from work, rode his bicycle to the Old Citadel Building on Marion Square, and reported to Carey Burts. At exactly one o'clock he was sitting in the outer office waiting to go in. He had spoken with Mrs. McConnell, who put him on notice that he had been under investigation and should be prepared to answer some questions about some boat oars and some fishing stuff. Also, she said, Mr. Burts had been in touch with Jake Burton, but she didn't know any more than that.

"That's fine," said Tee. "The oars and things belong to my daddy and I don't know a thing about Mr. Burton except that I don't like him. I heard that he got robbed. I don't know anything more than that except that I hope the robber got a lot of his money." He smiled at Mrs. McConnell.

"Don't say that inside, Tee," cautioned the lady.

"No, ma'am, I won't," he replied.

It was fifteen minutes later that Tee was summoned inside and went through the routine of standing respectfully in front of the desk with his cap in his hand. Carey Burts kept his back turned to Tee for a while before he swiveled around and began his questioning. He never invited Tee to take a seat, but that didn't matter either. Tee knew that he was being observed from the reflection in the same mirror that he had noticed before. He wondered if Burts knew that or if he thought it was a secret.

"I hear you have a boat," the gruff man said in a tone that was more like a question than a statement.

"Yes sir," answered the boy.

"How did you get a boat?"

"My daddy and I had it a good while," replied the boy, saying no more than was necessary.

"They tell me you have some oars and other fishing equipment."

"Yes sir."

"Where did you get them?"

"My daddy and I had those also."

"I was told that you stole them."

"Well, that's not true," replied Tee, still looking the inquisitor in the eye and still speaking in a soft, controlled voice.

"You know that I don't believe that for a second," said Burts.

Tee didn't reply but continued to maintain his poise and to look his antagonist in the eye. This didn't abate the mounting anger felt by Burts, who changed subjects, saying, "I suppose you don't know anything about what happened at Jake Burton's either?"

"Only what I heard," answered the boy, beginning to feel a certain satisfaction at the rising frustration betrayed in the voice of his questioner, but still poised and calm and keeping his eyes fastened on him.

"Don't get cocky. We have a way of finding things out and we'll get to the bottom of these things." Burts once again turned his back to Tee in order to study the boy's face in the mirror.

No, thought Tee, *he doesn't know that I am looking back at him.*

"Well, go out and make your report to Mrs. McConnell," ordered Burts.

Tee turned and left the room without changing expression until he sat before the desk of his friend. He looked into her face and presented a slight smile…a smile of satisfaction.

"It appears that the meeting went more to your satisfaction than his," said the kind lady softly, returning the same slight smile. They were both aware that Burts was probably watching them closely and that he could punish either of them if he thought they were allied against him.

"Sign this report here," Mrs. McConnell told Tee, and slid the clipboard with a pen attached across the desk to the boy, who signed where she had marked. He slid the clipboard back and again exchanged a friendly look with the lady. He was preparing to leave when Burts spoke from the doorway.

"Mrs. McConnell, give him the name and address of the detective I want him to go and see now."

"I don't have that, Mr. Burts," she said.

"OK," he said and went back into his office, returning with a paper in his hand. "Detective Tillman, he's at the station on Saint Philip Street. He's expecting him." He spoke as if Tee was not in the room, but his voice was still affected by his agitation with Tee.

"Yes sir," said the lady, who wrote the information on a slip of paper and handed it to Tee.

* * * * *

Tee rode his bike up Calhoun Street to Saint Philip Street, leaning it against the rack in front of an old, fortress-looking building, and walked inside. The sergeant at the desk was writing in a book, so Tee stood and waited until he was finished and looked at him. He said, "I'm supposed to see Detective Tillman. My name is Tee McLauren and I've been sent by Mr. Burts, the probation officer."

"Have a seat over there," said the sergeant, pointing toward a row of straight-back chairs lined up against the wall. Tee did what he was told and sat down, wondering how long this would take because he had told Leon he would be right back.

It was close to two o'clock when an athletic-looking middle-aged man came in the door. He looked like a movie version of a detective: brown suit and hat, with a bulge on the hip revealing the fact that he carried a .38 caliber police revolver.

"Detective, this young man is here to see you," said the desk sergeant.

Tillman stopped and looked at Tee. "Come with me," he said and led the boy down a hall and up a flight of old, creaky stairs to his sparsely furnished office.

"Sit down, son," said the detective courteously to the now apprehensive boy who had followed him into the room. "What am I supposed to talk to you about?"

"Mr. Burts, my parole officer, sent me," said Tee. "I am Tee McLauren."

"Oh," replied the detective. "You're the young man who got caught up in a brawl at Jake Burton's. You were helping your father. Too bad you and your dad didn't hit them harder." He smiled slightly and leaned forward. "Your dad is a good man and I hate what happened. He probably would have got off if he hadn't pled guilty. I tried to talk him out of it. He was embarrassed and felt guilty; I don't know why. Probably just from being there. He hated that you got caught up in it. I think that was the biggest problem."

The detective leaned back in his chair, studying the face of the young man. "Anyway, Burts wants me to quiz you about the robbery at Jake's. He thinks you either did it or know who did. Were you at Jake's the day of the robbery?"

"I haven't been through that door since I got arrested," said Tee.

"You've gotten bigger since all that happened. You must have liked it in Florence," the detective said with a grin.

'Well, sir," Tee said in his practiced, respectful voice, "the best part about Florence was leaving it, and I don't know why Mr. Burts thinks I was involved in the thing at Jake Burton's."

"Well, son, I've got a full caseload and I don't plan to take on too much extra work to benefit Mr. Burton and his motley crew. I don't see you as a suspect, so don't worry about what I'm going to do." Tillman glanced down at his desk. "Oh. By the way, how do you know Mr. Manigault?"

"He's a nice man who has been friendly to me. He's a good friend of Mannie Simmons on Chapel Street," Tee replied.

"Oh, yeah, I know Mannie Simmons. He's a good man too. You have good friends and that's a good sign. I'd trust their judgment over Carey Burts's any day," said Tillman as he got up from his chair and led Tee to the door. They shook hands. Tillman supplemented the handshake with a warm smile.

"Go on back to work and I'll speak to your boss if you have a problem from being late," said the detective. He watched the boy walk down the hall, thinking, *He's athletic enough to have done it and, if he did, I hope he got some compensation to make up for what all of that cost him and his family.* He smiled as he remembered Tee had said he had not gone through the door of Jake's but had said nothing about going through the roof.

Back on the street, Tee pedaled quickly back to the dock in time to fix a sandwich and return to work. He felt relieved after talking with Detective Tillman and knew that Burts was fishing in the dark. If he had known anything for certain he would have put Tee on the first train back to Florence. Tee also got some comfort from knowing that neither Miss Charlotte nor Leon would willingly give him away. He also knew that he had been honest with the detective: he had not walked through the door at Jake's since the night of the melee.

Leon and Tee enjoyed their lunch on the dock. The fact was that being late hadn't made any difference.

* * * * *

That same afternoon, Detective Tillman picked up the phone and made a call. "Let me speak with Mr. Burts, please," he said.

Chapter 18

Back at Mannie's

Mannie paused with the story, got up from the sofa and looked at his watch. "I guess we've had enough for today," he said, and walked over to the shed and started to shell some corn for the chickens.

George watched for a moment, then he picked up an ear and started to shell some corn too. He caught on quickly and laughed, saying, "I guess you're going to make a farmer out of me too."

"Not likely," said the old man. "It's a lot more to learn than just shelling and shucking. Don't forget, the farmer has to raise the corn too." He looked at the reporter. "When can we get together to finish this story?"

"Whenever you say. You've got my interest up. What did Detective Tillman say to Mr. Burts?"

"I'm not sure, but whatever he said sure did help Tee. When he reported in after that he only had to talk to Mrs. McConnell. It became routine. Frank and I never discussed it either. I'm sure that Frank simply let the police know that he had an interest in the boy. He didn't need to say a lot more."

"How long did that last?" asked the reporter.

"Burts didn't disappear," said Mannie, "but he stayed in the background watching. Tee had no doubt that his adversary still had plans to ship him off again, so he kept his guard up. Tee could feel his position getting stronger. He was making some money, saving some and investing some. Burts had good instincts; he saw that the boy's position was stronger and that it wasn't wise to move against him at that time."

Mannie paused, musing. "It's funny about bullies and gossips; they pick on people they perceive as being weak. But they need to be reinforced by others and don't like to go out on limbs alone. I suspect that Lt. Tillman let Burts know that Tee had friends in high places."

"Do you think Tee robbed Jake?"

Mannie answered, "The law presumes everyone to be innocent. Mannie Simmons does too. I go farther than that with my friends…I even defend them when they're charged. I don't ask them questions either." He looked the reporter in the eye. "You know that you can't write anything in your article that accuses Tee."

"I won't do that," the reporter promised. "What happened to Tee after that?"

"He was industrious, and he saved his money too. Not long after he went to work at the dock, he and Leon started mending and repairing boats in their off time. Rowboats and sailboats, things without engines. They would locate a boat in bad shape and fix it up and sell it. They sold seines and cast nets too. Some of the firemen made the nets at work and Tee would sell them for a commission. Charlie Rowland showed up at the dock one Saturday afternoon in work clothes and joined in. He had connections and brought in small sailboats for repair work. He would sail them around the Battery to the dock. Tee and Leon were impressed because neither of them could sail."

The reporter asked, "Did Charlie and Tee become good friends?"

Mannie smiled. "You know what Charlie had in mind. Mary couldn't continue to ignore a friend of her brother. He and Tee did admire each other but they had little in common aside from Mary."

"What did Tee do with his money?"

"He saved and invested in his little business. About once every month or so he caught the train and visited his cousin Henry, the lawyer. It was all business because Tee had little interest in socializing."

"What was happening with Mary?"

"OK, sit back down and we'll talk some more," Mannie said. "Charlie was determined and clever too. I also think he was being coached by a little lady on Judith Street…"

Chapter 19

Courtship

A week after they worked in the garden, Charlie began his campaign. He showed up on Saturday afternoon at the dock where Tee and Leon were repairing an old bateau. It needed some new wood on the sides and bottom and since it was made of cypress Leon thought it wasn't going to be easy to find. Good cypress is scarce and it's expensive when you find it. Charlie offered to invest in the project, but Tee said he knew where he could find some. It was tucked away in his mental inventory of an old shed on Judith Street.

Charlie didn't arrive at the dock until afternoon because of the Saturday parade at The Citadel so he couldn't launch his campaign with Mary's brother until all of that was over, but he had deployed his forces on two fronts. At ten o'clock, when the cadets were marching out for the weekly parade, a young man leaned his bicycle on the fence at 28 Chapel Street, quickly mounted the stairs to the second floor, and knocked on the door. The Saturday chatter was already starting so he had to knock several times before someone answered. It was Essie who came to the door. "Can I help you?" she asked.

"Would you deliver this to Miss Mary McLauren and tell her I also have a message?" he asked. "I'll wait." Essie disappeared into the house and he could hear her calling for Mary. Then a lot of new chatter began while the package was unwrapped, and a box of expensive chocolates was opened. Mary came to the door but before she could speak, the messenger began to sing:

Girl of my dreams, I love you, Ohh, honest I do…

Everyone in the house crowded to the door standing behind Mary, and when the messenger had finished his last note they applauded loudly. Mary blushed and smiled happily. She also noticed there was no card attached to the gift and no sign of Charlie. The messenger left without saying anything else or giving any clue as to who had sent him. There was a lot of speculation, but Mary didn't give any indication that she either knew or cared. Essie simply looked at her friend and smiled.

That afternoon when Mary and Essie went to Walgreens soda fountain, there were several Citadel cadets seated in a booth, but Charlie wasn't one of them. When the girls looked their way, the cadets waved and smiled but didn't come over. They spoke to the girls as they left…but they left.

The next Saturday it was early afternoon when a van pulled up in front of the house on Chapel Street and six cadets got out carrying brass musical instruments. They assembled just inside the gate and began to play. Mrs. Timmons was among the first to come on the porch and when she looked to the side yard there was a good crowd of neighbors standing about listening, including Miss Charlotte. The music had been chosen to please the ears of the elderly ladies, beginning with "I'll Take You Home Again, Kathleen," followed by "When Irish Eyes Are Smiling," and concluding with another rendition of "Girl of My Dreams."

When they finished, Mrs. Timmons summoned them into the house, where they were treated to chocolate and coconut cake. The young men enjoyed the treats and, more than that, they enjoyed the attention they received from the girls — young and old. Again, Mary blushed and smiled…and noted that Charlie was not present.

The campaign was underway, and the objective was surrounded. Following their usual procedure, the girls took their Saturday afternoon walk down King Street, walking through Kress's and Woolworth's, stopping to speak briefly with some of the salesgirls, and then they stopped at the soda fountain at Walgreens. Among the usual array of young people seated in the booths and at the counter were a few Citadel cadets…but Charlie was not one of them.

When Mary and Essie came home, there was a Citadel cadet sitting on the front porch of the boardinghouse talking with Mrs. Timmons. They were sipping coffee and he was munching on a generous slab of chocolate cake while they chatted. It was easy for them to amuse each other because they had such different backgrounds. Charlie knew funny things about prominent people and Mrs. Timmons knew a lot of equally funny things about people who weren't prominent.

Charlie was more than welcome because of the groundwork he had put in place that morning, following the script of the little lady on Judith Street. Mrs. Timmons was a gatekeeper who could open doors. But not only could she implement things, she could originate things. Mary saw this immediately and her admiration for the young man went up another notch. By this time, she also knew he had been working with Tee on the dock.

"Here, Mary, take my seat," said the landlady. "Essie, come with me and let's get Mary some cake and coffee. Charlie, would you care for more?"

"Some more black coffee, if you don't mind, ma'am. This cake is really good, and you gave me more than I needed. This is not a complaint, however," said the charmer.

It was easy for Mary to smile at the young man and to enjoy their conversation. Essie brought the coffee and cake and left them with the excuse that she was needed in the kitchen. A few minutes later, when Charlie suggested a walk around Charlotte Street, Mary accepted readily and they strolled up Alexander to Charlotte, enjoying the good spring day. They walked beside the high brick wall of the Second Presbyterian Church cemetery, stopped and studied the old tombstones and intricate wrought iron fence, then walked over to the Manigault mansion where they sat on a bench for a while and studied the unusual architecture of the old residence.

"I want you to go to a dance with me next week," Charlie said after a long silence.

"I can't," replied Mary. "I think you should know that I don't have a suitable dress to wear and that I have a family commitment that takes all of my attention."

"I know about that," Charlie replied. "Mrs. Timmons said she could make you a dress and some of the girls offered to help. A lot of people want you to go with me, but none of them as much as I do."

Mary's response was quick and emphatic. "Do you think I am going to let other people pay for my clothes? They like me, I know, but my family pays its own way."

"I know that," Charlie said. "Tee will pay for it."

"Tee?" asked Mary. "Where will Tee get the money?"

"Tee always has money," Charlie replied confidently. "He works all the time and knows how to make money. Don't say no until you talk with him."

"OK," she agreed. "I appreciate being asked and I also appreciate all the nice things you've done for me. I especially like the way you treated Essie at the factory. You're a good fellow and I like you. I just haven't included a social life in my plans."

"I know," said Charlie. "Talk with Tee first and then we'll talk again. Oh! By the way. Miss Charlotte has some nice things she wants to show you. You know, baubles and things." He laughed. Mary did too. It was a wide-reaching conspiracy — of the nicest kind.

* * * * *

It was Sunday after church and Mary was in Tee's room on Judith Street when her brother came in. She had swept and dusted and arranged everything neatly, as she always did.

"What brings you here, sis?" he asked.

"Have you been talking to Charlie Rowland about me?" she replied.

"If I talk with him at all, it's about you. You're all he wants to talk about," Tee said with a wide grin. "Yes, we talked about you going to a dance with him and I gave my permission."

"Your permission!" Mary said. "I don't need your permission. I'm the oldest member of the family here now and you listen to me, not the other way around." She spoke firmly, but with a grin wide enough to match her brother's.

"Sis, I have already given the money to Mrs. Timmons to buy the material for the dress and I have given some to Essie to buy some shoes and things," he said. "You're my family and you can't deny me the pleasure of doing something I really want to do for someone I love very much." Tee looked somewhat embarrassed as he said this, being unused to speaking openly about his emotions.

After a pause, he continued, saying, "I know that we'll hear from Daddy soon. He has to get his life back under control and we both know that he will. He'll want the farm back and I'm trying to help him. Cousin Henry and I have been talking with the bank and I've been able to put up some of the money to buy it back. This will surprise and please you: Daddy has been sending money back to Henry to look after us and to try and buy the farm back. I told Henry that you and I were looking after each other and for him to put all the money on the farm. So, you see, I'm looking after you. If you want to make me happy, you should begin to put your personal life in order, and you can begin by accepting the friendship of a really nice fellow."

Mary was visibly touched, but also troubled. "You have grown, Tee," she said, her face serious. "Not just physically either; you think like a man should. Please don't do anything that would cause them to send you back to Florence."

Tee looked at his watch and reminded Mary that they had to be on time at Mrs. Timmons's for lunch. They had started down the stairs when Tee stopped and said that he had to check the door to the room. Mary said they had locked it, but Tee went back anyway and checked the door. Then he stretched a small string over the space between the door and the doorjamb and rejoined his sister. They raced down the stairs two at a time and landed on the street laughing and holding hands. It was another happy day.

* * * * *

That evening when Tee returned, the string over the door was broken. He knocked on the door of his neighbor's room and when the man came out, he asked, "Did you hear or see anyone at my room?"

"I heard some moving about in there about an hour ago and

thought it was you," replied the neighbor.

"Did you see anyone?" Tee persisted.

"No, but I looked out on Judith Street a little later and saw a big man walking down toward America Street. Never seen him before. Walked like a baboon."

"Thank you," said Tee. "You've been a big help."

Tee unlocked his door and looked around his room. Everything seemed in order but after about thirty minutes of searching he found what he was looking for. It was a bank bag and it was hidden behind the folding card table leaning against the wall in the dark side of the room. His question was answered; he was being set up. Now he only had to figure out what to do about it.

The next morning, early, he went to Saint Philip Street to see Detective Tillman. Thirty minutes later he left the police station and went to work at the dock. Leon was busy when he arrived, and Tee told him that he had to report to the police and that was why he was late. It was good to have a friend at work. In fact, Tee was beginning to feel grateful that he had so many friends.

Chapter 20

Search and Seizure

Tee came straight from the dock to his room and arrived to find three men standing at his door talking with his neighbor. When he walked down the hall to where they stood, he recognized one of them as an employee of Jake Burton. It was one of the goons he and his daddy had struck with chairs at Jake's joint on Calhoun Street. Tee walked up close to him and looked him steadily in the eyes, realizing he was several inches taller than the man but not near as wide.

"Can I help you?" he asked.

"Are you Tom McLauren?" asked one of the men.

"Yes. I'm Tom McLauren, Jr.," answered Tee.

Showing his badge, the man said, "We have a warrant to search your apartment. Will you let us in?"

"Sure," said Tee.

"I'm Detective Sergeant Junkins and this is my partner, Detective Jacques. This man represents Jake Burton, who obtained the search warrant," the man continued.

"I know him," said Tee.

"Is it alright for him to come in while we search?" asked Junkins.

"Yessir. Don't leave him in the hall. We aren't allowed to put trash in the hall, so bring him in," said Tee, staring the goon in the eyes as he spoke.

"You'd better watch your mouth, kid," growled the goon. "It ain't safe to talk to me that way."

"OK, I'll watch my mouth and I'll also keep my eyes on you," Tee retorted. He stared in the goon's face with hostile eyes — and a smirk on his face.

"Knock it off," said the detective. "We've got a job to do here and this ain't helping. You two keep your mouths shut while Jacques and I conduct the search."

Tee opened the door and the four entered the room. The detectives set about their search. Tee took a seat but didn't offer one to the goon. After about thirty minutes, one of the detectives looked behind the folding table that was leaning against the wall and pulled out a bank deposit bag.

"Is this yours?" he asked Tee.

"No, sir," Tee replied.

"Do you know how it got here?"

"No, sir," said Tee.

"That's Jake Burton's deposit bag!" said the goon.

"How do you know?" asked the detective.

The goon took the bag and examined it. "It's his alright. He got it from the C&S Bank, and it has his initials down there in the corner," he said, pointing to the letters JB initialed in dark blue ink in the lower right-hand corner of the bag.

"Are you sure those are Jake Burton's initials?" asked the detective.

"Oh, yeah," assured the goon, presenting his most truthful face and voice. "Jake always puts his initials on his personal things. I remember seeing those initials on the bag the night it was stolen. It's the same bag and that's what we're looking for."

"Are you sure you don't know how this bag got here?" the detective asked again, holding the bag in his hand and looking at Tee.

"It doesn't belong to anyone here. It was either here when we rented the room, or someone put it here," Tee said.

"Who do you think would do that?" the detective asked.

"Somebody in this room. Not you, not Mr. Jacques, and not me. That leaves the ugly man standing over there," said Tee, turning in his chair to look at the goon.

"You're a little thief and you're going back to Florence!" said the ugly man, trying to contain his anger.

"Well, there's no reason to stay here," Detective Junkins said. "We've finished what we had to do, and I don't want to have to separate you two. You're not under arrest, Mr. McLauren, but don't leave town. You're also on probation so don't forget that either. We'll schedule a time for you to come in. Same thing for Mr. Burton," he added, turning to the goon. "Tell him we'll be in touch and set a time to come to the station house."

Tee never got out of his chair until the detectives started for the door, then he got up, opened the door for them and watched as the three men went down the stairs. The goon looked back at Tee with a smug grin on his ugly face. Tee gave him the same hostile glare he had previously offered, but when he shut the door he smiled.

* * * * *

It was one-thirty on the following Thursday when Tee entered the office of Detective Tillman. He was exactly on time but the last to arrive for the meeting. Jake Burton, the goon, Carey Burts, Lt. Tillman and a stenographer were all seated around the room when Tee came in; he took the only seat left.

Tillman switched on the intercom and asked Detectives Junkins and Jacques to join them. "Have you got the bag you took from Mr. McLauren's room on Judith Street?" he asked when the detectives arrived.

"Yessir," replied Detective Junkins, handing the bank bag to his superior.

"Mr. Burton," said Tillman, "can you identify this bag?"

Burton took the bag, looked it over inside and out and said, "This is the bag that was stolen from my residence behind the shop on Calhoun Street."

"Are you sure?" asked the detective.

"Positive," said Burton.

"How can you be positive?" asked the detective.

"It's one I got from C&S Bank and have used for years. It's got my initials on it right here," Burton said, pointing to the letters JB printed in dark blue ink on the lower right-hand corner of the bag.

"Who put those initials on the bag?" asked the detective.

"I did myself," said Burton.

"Thank you, Mr. Burton," said the detective, turning his face to Tee. "Mr. McLauren, have you ever seen this bag before?"

"Yessir," said Tee, noting the smug smiles on the faces of his accuser and the goon.

"When did you see it before?" he asked.

"When I put it behind the folding table in my room," said the boy.

"So, you admit you stole my money!" said Burton.

"No, but I admit putting the bag behind the folding table," said Tee.

Lt. Tillman opened the drawer of his desk and pulled out another faded green money bag with C&S Bank printed on the side and asked, "Have you ever seen this bag before, Mr. McLauren?"

"Yessir, that's the one I found in my room and brought to you two weeks ago. The one someone planted there," said Tee, looking at Jake Burton.

"Let me see that bag!" demanded the bar owner.

Lt. Tillman handed the bag to Jake Burton. All eyes were on him as he examined it in detail.

"Is that your bag?" asked Tillman.

"You're trying to confuse me," Burton said.

"Is that your bag?" the detective asked again. "That's all I want to know."

Burton looked around the room, glancing nervously from one to another as if to assess whether or not they believed. "I believe it is," he said. "It looks like it. Yes. I know it's my bag."

"There are no initials on this bag," Lt. Tillman pointed out.

"Yeah, I know, but it's my bag and it's the one that was stolen from me," the bar owner said.

"You just finished saying that the other one was the one that was stolen from you," said the detective. "Think about it. Are you sure now that this is the one?"

"I know what you're doing," Burton accused. "You're trying to confuse me and protect that boy. Well, he stole my money and it was in one of these bags. I know it was him and so do you." He spat out the words in anger at the detective, repeating, "You're trying to confuse me and protect him."

Tillman spoke quietly, measuring his words, and staring at the bar owner. "The question for us to answer here today is whether you want to go to court and swear that the bag found in Mr. McLauren's room was yours and the one stolen from you. If you want to go further, you can swear out a warrant for his arrest, and we'll start legal proceedings. I have to remind you that everyone in this room has been a witness to your confusion and I will certainly testify to what I have seen."

Carey Burts had worn a wide grin when Tee first admitted that he had put the bag behind the table, but the smile had faded as the additional facts were revealed. In the end Burts became a quiet spectator to the drama in the room and gave every indication that he would rather be someplace else.

After a few moments of silence, Tillman said, "Alright, this meeting is adjourned, and everyone can go. Mr. Burts, would you stick around after they leave so we can talk some more?"

"Yessir," said Burts.

* * * * *

After everyone but Burts had left, Tillman sat at his desk

shuffling papers and ignoring the parole officer until the door opened and Major Frank Manigault entered.

"You know Major Manigault, don't you?" asked Tillman.

"Yes, of course. Everyone knows Major Manigault," sputtered Burts nervously.

"Well, I'll leave the two of you to talk," said Tillman, standing up and walking out the door.

There was a moment of quiet as the two men looked at each other. The Major continued to stare intently, but Burts eventually dropped his gaze and looked at the floor.

"Let's get straight to the point, Mr. Burts," said the Major, speaking in a low, firm voice. "You seem to be more interested in putting Tee McLauren back in reform school than in helping him get rehabilitated. We both know that you're supposed to help and guide him and we both know that you haven't done that. Well, he'll probably do very well without your help so I'm not going to suggest that you go out of your way to reform him. I am, however, going to warn you against trying to hurt or harm him in any way."

Burts sat mutely staring at the older man, giving him his full attention.

"This conversation will remain between the two of us and will not leave this room unless you force me to publicly support the young man," the Major continued. "Do we have an understanding?"

"We understand each other," said Burts.

Chapter 21

Gumbo

That evening Mannie and the Major combined talents to prepare a seafood gumbo and were observing the ritual of a cordial Scotch before they put on their aprons. Their conversation centered on the events of that afternoon at the police station and, of course, the role of their young friend. Mannie was lounging back on the old leather sofa and Frank was relaxing in the chair.

"Do you think Tee robbed Burton?" Mannie asked.

"I don't know," replied the Major. "It would be a kind of poetic justice for the McLaurens to be compensated for the trouble Burton has caused them and it would only be just for Burton to suffer a little at their hands."

"Well, I hate for Tee to violate the law, but I agree with you about the justice of it," said Mannie. "You know what I mean, though; you just can't take the law in your own hands. We all disagree with the law sometimes."

"Yeah. You and I might disagree, but we generally comply. Tee's different. He writes his own rules. We both know that you can't get away with that for long, but he's willing to pay the price and doesn't ask for advice. When he went to Florence he didn't complain, he just went and did the time. He defines things for himself," said the Major.

The old man paused for a moment then added, "We have what we call a system of justice. Some lawmakers get together, they debate and argue, and finally write laws which represent their consensus. There's a lot of compromise involved in the process and the finished product is far from ideal. The courts interpret the laws and modify or change them when they apply it in the judicial process. The courts talk about substantial justice which means, I guess, that this is the best we have, and we just have to live with it. It seems that our young friend feels that he has the right to define these things for himself. It's been my observation that when he takes something from someone, he puts something back. It's a sort of balancing of the books. He sees something that's not being used, and he puts it to use and he replaces what he takes with either goods or services that benefit the other person."

"You make him sound like Robin Hood," laughed Mannie.

"Well, look at it this way. He is following a system of equity that seems fair to him. Robin Hood took from the rich and gave to the poor; Tee takes from both. He's not biased when it comes to teefing anything," said the Major, adding his laughter to Mannie's.

"I just hate to see him heading for trouble," Mannie said.

"You know, Mannie," said the Major, "this boy's world became unglued. His mother held it all together and when she died the family fell apart. Tom McLauren was a good, hard-working, strong man but he lost all of that. Mary was a nice, pleasant, hard-working young woman and she still is. She suffered but she remained pretty much the same. She is committed to putting her family back together, but she is still the same person she was when all of this happened. Tee was changed almost totally. He was a quiet boy who went about living the easy way. He did what he was told to do and didn't worry about how things were or how they got that way. The impact of his mother's death turned him into a man. Even as a boy he became the man of the family. He keeps his own counsel, doesn't ask for advice, and is always thinking. He looks for opportunities to make money and he takes advantage of them when they appear."

The Major paused for a moment, sipped on his Scotch, and looked into the fire reflectively. "You asked if I thought that Tee robbed Burton. I think he did. I also think he doesn't see it as a crime or a sin. To him it's justice to make someone pay when they do harm to others; to him it's fair to take money from Jake Burton and apply it toward the repurchase of the family farm."

"The police don't seem inclined to punish him," Mannie said. "Whether they want to protect him, or they just don't want to help Burton is the question. You said that every man has to decide what's right or wrong. That's true, but when the police come, they make that decision, they look at the facts and when they have them, they tell you if you're right or wrong. The only definition that counts then is theirs. That's how Tee ended up in Florence and his daddy in the state penitentiary." He stood up and began heading to the kitchen. "Oh, well, I'm getting hungry and we can talk about this later."

Tee came up the alley just as the two chefs began to prepare the meal.

"Hello, Tee," said the Major. "You're just in time. To be a member of this club you have to cook and tonight your apprenticeship begins."

"Are you fixing the roux?" the Major asked Mannie.

The big, heavy iron skillet was already on the gas range. "Yeah. I've got the lard and flour ready to put in the pan. Tee can stir it."

As Tee joined him at the range, Mannie cautioned, "This is important. Stir it constantly and watch it until it gets dark brown. It'll burn if you aren't careful and you'll get kicked out of the club before you ever get in."

"Are you sure you trust me with this job?" asked Tee.

"Sure, you're being tested. If you can't cook a roux, you aren't a cook. Besides, if you mess it up, we can start over," the Major said, giving reassurance to the novice.

"I peeled the shrimp and made a stock earlier today. I boiled the shrimp shells in this pot of water and seasoned it with celery, onion, and parsley. The salt and pepper are in the stock," said Mannie.

The Major proceeded to chop more onions and celery and chatted with Mannie as he worked. "What all do you want to use? Shrimp and oysters, of course. Do you want to add crabmeat too?"

"Sure. It's a seafood gumbo and I've got all of that ready. Let's use it all," Mannie replied, grinning and taking a sip from his glass of good single malt Scotch the Major had brought to the party.

Tee was stirring anxiously and studying the mixture in the heavy skillet. He kept looking at his two friends for support, but they had their backs to him and left him to sink or swim on his own.

"It looks brown now," Tee said.

The Major looked in the skillet and said, "Another minute or two," then he winked at Mannie and the two returned to their conversation, leaving the nervous young man to proceed on his own with what he knew to be the key to the flavor of the gumbo.

Another minute passed and Tee said, "It's ready," and he removed the skillet from the flame. Mannie checked it and agreed. They reduced the heat and added the chopped celery and onion and helped the novice to sauté the ingredients until they were soft.

"We're building it now, Tee," said the Major as he added the seafood stock gradually and took over the stirring until it came to a smooth consistency. "We'll let it simmer for about ten minutes." Tee continued intently watching, relieved that he was no longer at the controls.

"What next?" asked the boy.

"We'll add the shrimp, crabmeat, and green onions and keep on cooking over a low heat until the shrimp are tender. Do you want to add okra?" the Major asked Mannie.

"Sure. It's not a gumbo without okra," Mannie answered.

"Mannie is a purist, Tee," the Major said to the boy as he added the okra to the mix.

The process came to a finale with the addition of oysters and parsley. When the oysters began to curl, Frank added filé and they were ready.

"Is the rice ready, Mannie?" the Major asked.

"All ready."

"OK, let the festivities begin," said the Major raising his glass of Scotch to Mannie who also raised his drink. After clinking their glasses and downing the last of the Scotch, they served the gumbo over rice accompanied with glasses of cold Chardonnay.

The three seated themselves at the table and the conversation ceased and was replaced with *uhms, mmms,* and other sounds of satisfaction. It was several minutes before Tee broke the silence.

"I think the roux is the key to the whole thing and I've become a roux chef," boasted Tee.

"Maybe we have found a budding genius, Mannie," said the Major.

"I don't know about the roux chef, but before the night is over you will earn a reputation as a washer of dishes," said Mannie. "You can use my apron," he added.

They laughed and again concentrated on the gumbo.

About the time they had eaten their fill, the Major's driver came walking down the alleyway and Tee served him a generous plate of gumbo. Tee washed the dishes and the two friends sat and talked. When the driver had finished eating, the party broke up and he and the Major walked back up the alley to Chapel Street and the car. Tee finished his chore of washing and putting the dishes and pots and pans away, then came over and poured himself and Mannie a fresh cup of coffee and sprawled out contentedly on the sofa.

"Tee," Mannie said, "you'd better be careful. Burton and his goons aren't through with you and you know what that means. They know that the law isn't going to side with them so they're going to do what they know best. They'll hurt you if they can."

"I know," Tee replied. "My neighbor has seen one of the goons in the area and we know he can pick the lock on my door."

"Why don't you change the lock?" asked Mannie.

"I don't have anything in there he would steal and if he comes in my room, he may regret it," said the young man in such a serious voice that Mannie turned and studied his face intently for a minute.

They sat in silence for several minutes more before Mannie

spoke up. "Tee, it's one thing to be Robin Hood…but something altogether different to be Jesse James," he said. "Like I said, be careful."

A little later Tee said good night and left with Mannie's words in his mind.

Chapter 22

A Visitor

Tee was cautious now, wherever he went and whatever he was doing. Going through the railroad lot and the junk jungle, he was alert to every sound and movement in the brush around him. He carried a heavy wooden stick with him, even when he rode his bicycle. The stick was about four feet long and three inches around and when he was just sitting around, he would carve on it with his pocketknife. Before long, it started to shape into an ornate piece of oak sculpture: a dog's head at the handle and intricate designs along the shaft, and with a polished and stained surface it attracted attention. People would ask him where he got it and where they could get one like it. He gave one to Mannie and one to Frank Manigault, who prized them and recommended that Tee make some to sell.

Thus, Tee and Leon had found another enterprise to work on when their boat business was slow. It turned out that Leon had talent in wood carving, and he became more efficient and artistic the more he worked. As with most things we are good at, Leon also enjoyed the work. Tee always seemed to have access to the raw materials and Leon, who had come to rely on Tee's resourcefulness, never thought anything about where they came from. They called their product a hiking stick, but Tee wasn't a hiker, unless you consider walking through the junk jungle hiking. Tee got comfort from his stick and he kept one by his bed at night.

He was cautious, but he wasn't afraid. He still went everywhere he wanted to go, but he warned Mary and Essie to be careful themselves and let him know if they saw anyone suspicious hanging around the boardinghouse. The girls never went out at night unescorted, so Tee didn't worry too much about that, but he told Charlie Rowland as another measure of caution. Several times he thought he saw someone watching him from across Judith Street, but he couldn't be sure. At night he relied on the regular lock on the door and would simply lock up when he went to bed, but he also put a string of empty cans around on the floor and disabled the light switch on the wall. He slept well...but he was a light sleeper.

It was three o'clock one morning when he heard someone attempting to open the door. He picked up his stick and moved silently away from the bed so that he was positioned behind the door when it opened. A shadowy figure tiptoed in and got caught up in the string of cans which rattled around making a loud noise.

"Dad blame it, Tee!" said a familiar voice and the shadow clicked the light switch unsuccessfully and tossed a seabag into the center of the room.

This headed off any offensive action by Tee, who switched on the light to see his daddy standing in the middle of the tin cans, puzzled but smiling at his son.

"Well, Tee, I'm home," Tom McLauren said unnecessarily.

After greeting each other with big hugs and slaps on the back, they brought Tom's big suitcase in from the hall and decided that sleeping was out of the question, so they walked to the all-night chili parlor on King Street next to the Francis Marion Hotel and joined the few other night people at the counter.

Mike, the counterman, was a fellow everyone knew. Mike, on the other hand, didn't know anyone's name and it didn't matter. Not many knew his last name and that didn't matter either. When you called out the name "Mike," you would have his attention. He didn't need to know your name because he never tried to get the attention of his customers. He worked in a white T-shirt with the sleeves rolled up, revealing an exotic display of the kind of tattoos seamen picked up in foreign ports, and he kept his cigarette pack rolled up in one of the sleeves. His trademark was a Lucky Strike dangling from his lips with a long ash extending and hovering over the chili. He never flicked the ash and it was a constant concern of the diners that it would eventually end up in their bowls. It never happened that way. For some mysterious reason, the ash would always fall at Mike's feet, to the amazement and relief of the diners.

Mike never smiled nor engaged the customers in conversation beyond that necessary to take their orders or their money. He made an exception when the McLaurens walked in, an event that was noted by the other diners, who turned to look at the special guests. Chili was served with Oysterette crackers and strong black coffee. If the excitement of the night wasn't sufficient to keep the reunited father and son awake, the coffee would be.

They talked and laughed and discussed the events in each of their lives and naturally the conversation came around to Mary. Tom was unhappy that she had quit school the year before, but he wasn't surprised. He didn't like her working in the cigar factory because he thought the work was too hard for her but came to agree with Tee, who reminded him that Mary wasn't a little girl and that she always knew how to work hard.

They went back to Judith Street, where they talked until six o'clock, when they noticed the time and decided to go to the boardinghouse and greet Mary and the others at breakfast. When they arrived a few minutes later they went into the kitchen, where Mrs. Timmons was busy rolling dough for biscuits. She dropped everything and greeted Tom with a dusty hug, leaving doughy handprints on his shirt. She made such a racket that some of the girls ran in and, upon seeing Tom, raced back to get Mary.

The reunion was loud, emotional and from the heart. It was not easy for Tom to talk Mary into going on to work and he was successful only because he convinced her that he needed sleep and would see her after she got off that afternoon. He and Tee drank more coffee as the others ate breakfast and Tom walked to the factory with the girls as Tee walked to the dock. Tom came back to Judith Street and fell exhausted into bed, where he slept for eight hours straight. He was wakened by Mary's knock on the door.

The second reunion centered on the large suitcase, which he opened to show the gowns and dresses he had picked up for his daughter. She tried them on and swayed around the room to the compliments freely offered by her first admirer. The question of what to wear to social events with Charlie was more than solved.

"How did you know my size?" she asked.

"Don't be silly," he replied.

Chapter 23

Making New Plans

The McLauren reunion continued for two days as Tom revisited family and friends and turned over in his mind his plan to repurchase the farm and return home. Charlie Rowland liked the father of the girl who was becoming more and more the center of his life, and Tom was comforted by the strong, intelligent man who wanted very much to be the protector of his daughter.

Tom now knew that his children were doing well. He had worried about them the whole time that he was gone. He was ashamed of the way he had reacted to his wife's death. He felt weak and that he had not been a responsible parent just when he was needed most. The drinking, which culminated in his going to prison and Tee being sent to Florence, caused him the most shame. He was led to reflection and prayer as he had looked out from the deck of his ship at the vastness of the ocean.

Quit feeling sorry for yourself. It didn't just happen to you. Be responsible to your children. These thoughts and others circled around in his head until he was ultimately able to sort them out and rearrange his life.

His job gave him a steady source of income and he purchased insurance through his union. He arranged to have most of his money sent to Cousin Henry for the children and to establish an account, which he planned to use to make his purchase of the farm. He came home renewed and ready to truly fill his role as a parent. The strength he saw in his children surprised him. It also pleased him greatly…but he was puzzled by Tee and concerned that he might be headed back to trouble. He also wanted Mary to finish high school.

A few days after he came home, he purchased a ticket on the Coast Line so he could meet with Cousin Henry, but before he left, he had a family meeting with Tee and Mary. Tom talked slowly and earnestly to his children, who studied his serious face as they listened.

"I want both of you to know that I'm well now and fully able to deal with anything that might come up. You don't need for me to tell you how embarrassed I am for having been weak when we all needed me to be strong, but that's behind us now. The two of you were more than strong. You took up the slack while I was away, but I'm back now and ready to be the head of this family. What does that mean? It means that I will repurchase your mother's farm so that we'll at least have that. We can't get her back, but we can try to be positive about her memory and the farm will always be hers."

He turned to his daughter. "Mary, I want you to finish school. I'll talk with the high school principal and see what we can do to get your diploma. If we can take a shortcut we will, but if we have to do the year over, we'll do that too. Charlie will soon be a college graduate and you will need to be educated too, even go to college if you want to do it."

Mary thought a moment and said, "I agree. I've been thinking about it and that's what I need to do. I haven't made plans to marry Charlie but, whether I do or not, I know that I want to be educated and to fit in with those who are. You talk with them and I'll do whatever they say."

Tom then turned to Tee and began, "Tee, just who are you, anyway?" and the three of them laughed.

"What can I say to you as your father?" Tom continued. "You've shown yourself to be a better man than I am, but I am older and more traveled than you, so that gives me something to stand on. The fact is that I have a fear that you walk too much on the other side of the street. Please don't let your guard down and get back in trouble. I know that it was my fault last time, but they have their eyes on you now. There's also the question of Jake Burton and his thugs; they aren't through with us yet."

Tee reflected quietly before he said, "Daddy, you don't owe us any apologies. We both know that it was more than you could stand to lose Mother. As hard as it was on us, we know that it was worse on you. We're glad you're back and we expect you to head up our family. We want to listen to your advice, and we'll follow it. And don't worry about me going back to Florence, I sure don't plan for that to happen. I also watch out for the goons and don't take chances with them or Burton. I avoid that part of Calhoun Street. If they want me, they'll have to come here and I'm alert — always."

With hugs all around, the meeting broke up and the three walked to Union Station, where Tee and Mary watched as the train pulled out and Tom headed back to where it all started. Three days later Tom showed back up in Charleston and held another meeting of his small clan in the room on Judith Street.

"Mary, it's lined up," Tom said. "You had good grades while you were there and the school, principal and teachers all want to assist you. If you go back immediately, they will arrange for you to make up for lost time and to take special tests that will qualify you for graduation. People like you, Mary, and understand. Are you willing to pack up and go?"

"I can go anytime but I do owe it to the people at the factory to give them notice, which I'll do tomorrow morning," she replied with apparent eagerness.

"Tee," said Tom, "you're next. As soon as Mary finishes school, I want you to start. You have real quality, but you don't want to stall out on this level. When Mary graduates, she can come back here and go to the College of Charleston while she rules over our household. I'll send money and you can both work part-time and we will make it very well. I was surprised at how much money you brought to Henry; he was too. He put it toward the purchase of the farm and, combined with my earnings, we now have a title to the farm in my name. We also have a mortgage, but it's manageable. Henry has rented the farm out and we have some income from it, especially the tobacco allotment, but not enough to make the payments. We owe him a lot."

"They sure were good to me," said Mary, "and I won't forget it."

The planning continued for a while, after which they went together to the boardinghouse for lunch. Three days later, Tom boarded a bus for New Orleans, where he met his ship and was back at sea. Mary rode the Coast Line and went back to school, where she would attend classes for what was left of the school year and receive special tutoring and a lot of testing.

After Mary left Tee felt really alone, and after spending some time in his Judith Street room, he wandered over to Chapel Street to visit his wise old friend, Mannie Simmons.

* * * * *

Charlie Rowland sat in his barracks room at The Citadel and looked at the picture of Mary on his dresser. She gave it to him at the same time she told him she was leaving. He felt a mixture of emotions and gravitated between the sadness of seeing her off on the train and the thrill of their first kiss. Ironically his first kiss was a goodbye. Goodbye or not, it sealed their relationship as far as he was concerned, and his mind settled on his strategic plan. Graduation from college was the key for both of them and that's what they were about.

He was proud of Mary and her family. Tom was a real man who had fought his depression and was able to come back strong. Mary was an exception. She walked into a room, a field, or a factory and she was always received the same: people liked her and wanted to be close to her. Tee was a mystery to everyone. His walls were up, and he was comfortably entrenched behind them. He was cordial enough to those he liked, and Charlie was pleased to be one of them, but Tee McLauren was out to make progress, not friends.

The family was scattered again, but they were reunited in a special way.

SUMMER 1941

Chapter 24

The Goons Return

Tee tried to avoid the hobos and their little section of the junk jungle. Motivated by necessity, they had shown more imagination than you would expect in designing and arranging their shelter. People who exist on their level of society aren't looking for "swank," but want to protect themselves from the elements with as little effort as possible, and that was what they had accomplished. A little removed from the junk piles, they had located their lair in a cluster of hedges that afforded them privacy. They covered their hideaway with an assortment of tin, wood, and canvas. It was a work in process and was never finished; whenever they found something that would work, they used it. They slept under the covered part and would huddle up there whenever the weather drove them to it.

To one side they had a cleared space where they could build a fire to cook over or to gather around for comfort. Tee thought to himself, *they're not stupid, they've been defeated by life, but not entirely; they've found a level of existence that they need to cling to, and they do.* From time to time Tee would drop off a package of something of use to them. Sometimes he would bring food and sometimes clothing or building material. He never mingled with them; in fact, he never had a conversation with any of them, which seemed to suit everybody. He also didn't know whether they even knew who was leaving the packages until one afternoon.

It was later than usual when he left the dock and allowed his thoughts to wander off to the extent that he was startled when he turned a corner in the junk pile and came face to face with an old, unwashed man who was standing in the middle of the path. Tee jumped back in surprise and then laughed as the old man did the same. The hobo laughed too.

"Son," said the 'bo, "we thank you for the things you bring to us, but we want to warn you that something's going on. We've seen two big and dangerous-looking men hanging around in the area and wanted to let you know. We know they aren't here on a mission of mercy and probably mean to harm someone. They're not railroad men either. We know all of them by sight. No, these birds are bad."

Tee had been surprised twice; the first surprise was the old man's unexpected appearance in the path and the second was the intelligence shown by his speech.

"Thank you, sir," said Tee respectfully and gratefully. "I know who they are, and you're right; they mean to do harm to me. Do you know where they are now?"

"They're not here now, but they've found a spot where they can conceal themselves and wait. I'll show you," said the man and motioned for Tee to follow as he led him to a spot close to the path but secluded enough to give the goons the concealment they wanted. They had pulled an old car seat into the spot where they could wait in comfort. It was something you wouldn't see unless you were looking for it: just a strip of brown cloth draped over a rusty automobile frame and so close in color that you would have to look closely to see it. When the goons were in the area the cloth appeared and it would disappear when they left. As they sat on the car seat and watched for Tee, they were being watched themselves by the old man, who had made himself a viewing spot that was equally as comfortable.

"You've helped me a lot and I thank you," said Tee as he looked the spot over and began to form a strategy of his own.

It gave the old man a renewed sense of relevance to be involved in the adventure and he refused when Tee tried to compensate him for his time and trouble.

"My time isn't worth anything to anyone, especially me. My colleagues enjoy sleeping more than I do," he said and again Tee was surprised by his vocabulary.

The game continued until one day, when he thought the time was right, Tee made himself vulnerable, or at least he appeared to be.

He'd seen the draped cloth on his way in, so he circled around the path going to the dock. At noon he started out the usual way and as he came to the spot where the goons were concealed, they let him go by, then jumped out behind him armed with knives. It was almost a repeat of the fight at Jake's, except that Leon had followed Tee. When the goons rose up behind him, they never saw Leon until he struck one of them on the head with his hiking stick. The other turned only to be struck behind his head by Tee, who was also carrying a hiking stick. The fight was over just like that, and the goons had lost the rematch.

Tee called and reported the incident in detail to Detective Tillman, who went immediately to Jake's. He arrived just in time to see Jake firing the goons. Tillman encouraged them to take a bus out of town. It didn't take much encouragement; they had lost face twice in the roughhouse business and Jake was disgusted. Goons are expendable. Their replacements were hired within an hour of their departure and Jake explained their duties. It was nothing complex, they simply did what they were told to do, and they had no input in the decision-making process. Jake fumed a while, but business was good and the first Saturday of the month, always the best, was coming up.

Saturday night was unusually active at the bar and when he closed the gaming room Jake followed his routine of counting his money in his private room and lounging in a full tub of hot water. He had his cigar and his whiskey, and the count had been good. He smiled as he enjoyed the luxury of his enterprise and felt proud of his success. He failed to see the shadowy form descend quietly and gracefully down a knotted rope from the skylight and move ninja-like across the outer room and pick up the bank bag from the dresser. As quickly and quietly as it descended, it climbed back up the rope and through the skylight and disappeared into the night.

* * * * *

Monday morning Detective Tillman appeared at the dock and, after looking around, accepted a cup of coffee from Leon and led Tee off to one side.

"Don't push your luck, Tee," he said to open the conversation.

The boy didn't spar with the man he respected so much.

"I think I know what you're saying. I try not to rely on luck too much," he said.

"No one is making a charge against you but we both know that you're a suspect for having robbed Jake Burton and we're talking about serious crime. You're on the wrong foot and it can only lead you back to prison. You're smarter than that and your family deserves better. Mary is headed in the right direction and so is your father. It's just you who's doing wrong." Tillman looked straight into the eyes of the boy as he spoke in his quiet but firm way.

There was a long silence, and then Tee said, "I'm certainly not saying that I robbed Jake Burton, but I won't pretend to be sorry that someone did. He sits on the sideline and sends dangerous people out to harm folks who only want to be left alone. So far, he hasn't been successful in his attacks on me and my family but that's not because he didn't try. If Leon and I hadn't been prepared for his goons, I wouldn't be talking to you right now. All they got was another knot on their hard heads, but they would have killed me, and you know it. You should be talking to Jake because I don't plan to keep waiting for him to succeed. Tell him that the next time he attacks anyone in my family he will personally pay the price." Tee said these things quietly and earnestly but with a respectful attitude.

"You've been more than a friend to us, Mr. Tillman, and we're grateful," he added. "I don't want to be a criminal and I certainly don't plan to go back to prison. Maybe Jake will listen to you...I know I will."

The detective finished his coffee in silence, continuing to study this most unusual young man. He didn't know why he made such an exception for someone he suspected strongly of very serious crime. It shouldn't matter that Burton precipitated all of it and deserved anything he got and more. The fact remained that his job was to uphold the law and to punish violators and he knew that he had come to a real bias in favor of the boy. He held the empty cup for a while and continued to reflect on the events of this case and how he had departed from his usual objectivity. It pleased him to see Burton punished and, he had to admit, for Tee to get away with doing it. Finally, he spoke.

"Tee, I don't want to keep repeating myself, but I want to give you this last warning: You stay away from Burton and his place of business. You said you hadn't been through the door of his joint; well, you had better stay off the roof too. You know I like you and your family, especially your father, but I'm in the law enforcement business and don't like making exceptions. Let's be friends and keep it that way. It would be painful for me to come after you, but I will, and you must know it. You're ahead of the game now and Burton probably won't bother you anymore. If you see anything to indicate that either you or Leon are threatened, just let me know. I'm pretty tough too and have a license to show it."

Tee listened intently as Tillman gave him advice which he knew he had to follow. All the things the detective had said were things he knew to be true. He was through with Jake. He had no more score to settle with him or his thugs. Tee had come to this conclusion even before the detective had come to see him but was glad to have had it so forcefully stated. It didn't hurt to hear it or to look into the serious face of the conscientious lawman.

"Thank you for everything you have done for us, and don't worry — as far as I'm concerned Jake is in another world and we won't see each other again," Tee said.

After shaking hands, Tee went back to his deck duties. Leon had spoken to the officer but had gone immediately back to his labors and made no attempt to get involved in the conversation.

"Thanks for the coffee, Leon," said Tillman and waved good-bye. He walked through the junk jungle on his way back to his car, which he had parked on Chapel Street. He avoided the hobos but thought to himself how unexpected things can happen with even the most unlikely people. *Who would have thought these people would ally with Tee? Who would even think that they were still capable of interaction of any sort?* He continued his walk in silent reflection and wondered,

How much do you suppose Burton paid this time? He sure was mad but I think he was a little frightened that the robber could come this close to him without being seen or heard and, of course, he knows that he could have done a lot more that take his money.

The following Saturday Leon opened a little trading post on Chapel Street and laid out the merchandise he and Tee had gathered, including two real fancy switchblade knives, only slightly used.

Chapter 25

Tee's Enterprises

It was late Saturday afternoon when Tee showed up at Mannie's. Leon was closing the trading post and business for their first day had been good. Their collection rate on boat sales and money lent was 100 percent. Tee was allowing Leon to buy a half interest in the business by letting him pay weekly, or when he had the money. Tee always knew when Leon had the money because he was the one who generated it, but he trusted and liked Leon and ultimately wanted him to own the entire business because he had other things in mind for himself.

They operated from a little storeroom on lower Chapel Street with a hand-painted sign hanging on the front.

FISHING GOODS STORE
Open all day Saturday

Mannie put down his newspaper. "What are you merchants selling now?" he asked Tee.

"We sell all kinds of fishing stuff, including bait, and are starting to show a pretty good profit selling reconditioned and new rowboats on credit. We've got three sold and are collecting on them every Saturday. A man on Columbus Street makes them and will sell them to us unfinished. Leon and I paint them, caulk them and get them ready to put in the river. Three people have ordered a boat as soon as we have one ready and we'll sell oars, oar locks, anchors, ropes and all kinds of nets and fishing stuff," Tee explained.

"How do you know these people will pay?" asked Mannie.

"We've sold three on credit and they haven't missed a payment yet," said Tee.

"You're lucky. You can easily get stuck. They can hide the boat and hide from you when you try to collect. You'd have a hard time getting your money or the boat back," Mannie said.

"We've got a system," Tee said. "We don't sell to anyone who can't get their preacher and one deacon from their church to guarantee the payment. It works."

"How did you come to know so much about church? You haven't been in a church since I've known you," Mannie asked as he brought Tee a cup of coffee and settled down on the big sofa with a cup of his own.

"I know more about church than you think. We're Presbyterian and went every Sunday back up home," Tee said. "Boys go to church because their parents make them go. Girls are different; Mary goes every Sunday. She's not only more religious than me, she's a lot nicer and sincere." He took a sip of his coffee. "I don't know where I stand right now, but I still know a lot about church. People want to look good in church and they surely don't want the preacher or the deacons coming after them."

Tee smiled at his friend and continued, "Besides, the people who buy these boats use them to make money. They sell crabs, shrimp, and fish so they need them and don't want to lose them."

They looked up the alley and saw Frank Manigault ambling their way, looking happy. He had his usual smile and there was a little more spring in his step, and he was moving the hiking stick Tee had carved for him in motion, not quite like a drum major, but with some exaggeration.

"Well, I'm glad to see both of my friends," the Major said. "I just decided to drop in and this is a pleasant surprise. Tee, tell me about your latest ventures. I'm told you are in the retail trade dealing in marine supplies and watercraft. How are you doing?" He spoke in a voice as exaggerated as his walk.

Tee and Mannie supplied the information about the business. Frank was impressed with the credit line and screening process.

"You may have hit on something, Tee. The church exerts a great deal of pressure on people and I agree with you that they have to look good on Sunday. Do you charge interest on the loan?" the old man asked.

"Yes, we charge interest on the money we lend but not on anything we sell," Tee replied. "We made enough profit on the sale, so we don't need to charge interest."

"I'm *really* impressed now," the Major said. "I've finally found someone who knows what enough is."

"Yeah," Mannie chimed in. "I'm probably better at it than most people. I don't worry about money and I like my time to myself, so I don't work more than I have to. But you, Tee, you're ahead of the game although you work too much and don't take much time for yourself. Being young you can do that for a while, but sooner or later some young girl is going to catch your eye and you'll start sitting around writing poetry and smelling flowers."

"Ha! Ha! Ha!" replied the young man with an exaggerated, sarcastic laugh. "I don't have enough time for that."

"He knows what enough is in some things and not in others," the Major observed, and they all laughed. They enjoyed each other's company for a few more minutes before the Major brought the subject around to the war in Europe.

"The Germans have headed into Russia. I'm surprised at that; you'd think Adolf would have more sense than that," he said.

"I was thinking the same thing," said Mannie. "Napoleon made that mistake and never recovered from it. The Germans move pretty fast, but Russia is big, and the winters are impossible. Tee, you'd better start learning to use a gun because Uncle Sam will be looking for you pretty soon. Miss Charlotte's boy is in the Army already and The Citadel boys are going on duty as fast as they graduate. That means Charlie Rowland will go right in."

"Yeah," said Tee. "You know Mary is back, she passed her exams and is now a high school graduate. She said Charlie wants to get married right away, but she wants to wait a while, and she got her old job back at the cigar factory." He looked pensive. "Things are changing. A lot of the young guys around here have gone to the Navy Yard as apprentices. If you're sixteen and pass the test, they put you in a program to teach you a trade. You get paid too."

"Are you going to do that, Tee?" asked the Major.

"No, sir. They don't pay much, and I need to make more than that. I've got several things working for me. We've got the farm back. We rented it out for now, but we need to pay the mortgages. I plan to work a little longer to get that done. Maybe I can go back to high school and maybe even college. Daddy and I want Mary to go to college this fall. She'll live with us and go to school. Before he left for New Orleans, we moved to 28 Chapel Street into an apartment on the third floor."

Tee looked down at the ground and said quietly and thoughtfully, "This will be Daddy's last trip to sea, and with the money he makes this time and what I've put up, we're in good shape. And I feel pretty certain Mary and Charlie have a future together."

"I know that, boy," the Major said. "They'll do well together. They both have good family trees," he added, winking at Mannie.

"I don't know much about Charlie's family tree, but Mary would be well advised to do a little pruning on hers," Mannie replied, looking at the Major instead of Tee. Then he winked at the boy to show he was joking.

After more good-natured exchanges, the Major said, "Walk with me to the street, Tee," and got up to leave. "Thank you again for your hospitality, Mannie," he added. He put his hand on Tee's elbow as they walked up the alleyway to Chapel Street.

When they reached the street, the Major said, "Why don't you come and visit my church some Sunday, Tee? We're Huguenot, which is not too different from Presbyterian. We're French Protestants and you're Scottish Protestants; both churches follow the Calvinist tradition. Think about it. We also have some pretty girls and some of them might be tolerant enough to be friends with you." He smiled as he spoke, but Tee detected a serious note in his voice. He responded in kind.

"Thank you, sir, for all you have done for me and my family. Your friends and family aren't ready for the likes of me and I'm sure there aren't many of your friends anxious to have this jailbird calling on their daughters. Maybe after the pruning or when I've cleaned up my act and made myself presentable, we can discuss this again." He laughed as he added, "You have the love and respect of a lot of people but even you shouldn't try to launch a social career for me. It'd be like invading Russia." The Major joined in his laughter.

Yessir, thought Tee. *I'm lucky to have good friends.* As he watched the distinguished old gentleman get in his car and drive off, he had another thought. *He didn't mention Jake Burton, so I guess he hasn't heard about it yet.*

✵ ✵ ✵ ✵ ✵

It was an unusual Sunday for Tee. He had nothing to do and slept in until he heard the familiar sales pitch of the black paperboy. *News and Courier* paper routes were delivered by white boys and the streets sales were conducted exclusively by blacks. The sounds were a part of the uniqueness of Charleston. Tee liked the sounds,the smells and the great old buildings; they were different from anywhere he had seen — which wasn't much — or even read about.

Git tha Sunday mornin noos…

Git tha Sunday mornin noos…

Git tha Sunday mornin noos an coooo….reee….oohh!

The Major said that call was right out of the opera *Porgy and Bess.* Tee wasn't sure about that except that if the Major said it, he believed it. The Major called it "singing commercials." Tee didn't have names for them, but he liked them; he especially liked Josie's.

Josie got shark steak…ain need no graveeee…

Put em in da pan and feed em to da babeeee…

There were others. They were all musical and expressed the original style of the peddler. They were called street criers and they peddled their goods and wares by singing out. Their carts and wagons were also decorated to express their individual style. Mannie would put a felt hat on his old horse during the summer-time when it got really hot. He cut holes in the hat for the ears to protrude through and, with the blinders shading the horse's eyes, it created a real fashion statement.

In addition, the children playing outside were always singing something:

Light fingator light…ah'll giv yu a peck a rice!

This was designed to induce a June bug, a bright green iridescent beetle, to stop so they could catch him and tie a piece of their mother's sewing thread around him and let him fly under their control. These bugs were easy to catch around the oleander bushes but that was because they liked the blooms and had little or nothing to do with the singing promises. After a while, they would be released, but they never got any rice. Tee was amused; they promised a peck of rice, but it was just another false promise.

Tee bought a newspaper and headed back up Chapel Street where he saw Mr. Thompson sitting on the low brick wall reading his paper. The old man looked up and smiled at Tee, whom he liked, but he mainly just wanted someone to listen to his opinions about the wars raging across the world and how it wouldn't be long before the United States would be in it. He predicted that the big threat to America was Japan. "They've forgot all about Jay-pan," he continued to preach, and everyone he preached to was more amused than alarmed.

"Major Manigault says that Hitler made a mistake going into Russia," Tee said, joining Mr. Thompson in conversation because he wanted to be courteous. The war was rarely on Tee's mind, but he knew that all the adults were consumed with it and he always made a point of listening. He was glad that he at least knew enough to join in the conversation with this curious old man.

"You know, boy, everybody laughs at Jay-pan and says that we can lick them with one hand tied behind our back," Mr. Thompson said. "The problem is that they're a lot tougher than that and we just might wind up with both hands tied behind our back."

"I don't know about them," Tee said honestly.

"Of course you don't…neither do the people who are running this country," the old man replied. "We've been struggling to keep food on our tables and haven't had time to study about these people who live halfway around the world from us, but the people who run our country should know and I'm afraid they don't."

"Well, some of our men are being drafted in the Army so we must be getting ready," Tee said.

"Oh, we'll get ready alright and our boys will be the best soldiers in the world after a while…but you pay a price for not being ready," Mr. Thompson said.

Tee sat on the wall with Mr. Thompson and thought about what he had said. The old man looked off for a while, took a chew of Red Mule, and went back to reading the paper. After a minute of silence Tee said goodbye and left him to his study of the news.

"Take care, son. I enjoyed talking with you," Mr. Thompson said.

Tee walked back to his room and read the paper and continued to think about the old man, who wasn't well educated but who captured his interest. *I'll have to ask Mannie or the Major about this,* he thought.

When he finished reading the paper, Tee went out on the third-floor porch and rocked in the chair that had been his mother's. He could look out over the rooftops of the adjoining houses and see the river and a good part of the railroad lot. A couple of firemen from the John Street Station were exercising the horses, which always fascinated Tee. These big and beautiful Clydesdales were the finest animals he had ever seen, and he envied the young black men who had charge of them. They waved at Tee when they saw him standing at the porch railing and he watched them go all the way down to the railroad lot before they turned around and returned the horses to their stalls. These men took great care of their animals, fed them well, groomed them, and kept their stalls clean, with fresh straw.

Tee had been at the station one day when the alarm sounded and watched as they hitched up to go to the fire, which was at the junk jungle. All of the harness was in place and attached to the traces so that one man would back the horse into position and the other would lower the traces onto the back of the horse and hook it under his belly. Then they were off. *These horses enjoy this as much as the firemen do,* thought the envious former farm boy.

He was lying back in the comfortable chair and rocking gently when Mary came in from church. "I'll fix us some lunch," she offered.

"No, let's walk down to Walgreens and get a sandwich," her brother replied. He took her hand and started down the stairs before she could argue about it.

Chapter 26

At Walgreens

Mary liked being with her brother and was especially glad that he invited her to lunch. They could be alone and talk. She liked to talk with her daddy and her brother, and it was seldom she had a chance. Her daddy was gone, and her brother was always busy doing something that required him to be away from her. She also was proud of this big and strong young man who didn't even own a dress shirt. He could afford one, but he only wore work clothes. It was not intended as a statement nor was it intended to set him apart from other people…it simply meant that he didn't try to impress others one way or the other.

Mary had to struggle to recall the little boy on the farm who was always anxious to please everyone, especially his mother. He had copied every move his daddy made and added to that some things that he admired about Rev. Conyers. She knew that he had changed overnight when he lost his mother, but how did he come to be a man so quickly?

As they walked up Charlotte Street by the Second Presbyterian Church where she had attended services a short time before, there were still a few people gathered by the gate.

"Mary, you decided to come back?" asked one of her girl-friends, talking to Mary but looking at Tee.

"No. My sweet brother has asked me to lunch," she said proudly and introduced Tee to the group.

Tee smiled and nodded graciously and with obvious confidence. This was one of the things Mary couldn't understand. He had no social contacts, yet he was so comfortable around others even when he was the only one not dressed up. Sometimes she thought it was because he was indifferent toward them and it didn't matter to him what they thought, but this wasn't a satisfactory answer because he was attentive and nice to others and was an excellent listener. *No,* she thought, *he's a mystery to me, but I love him.*

They crossed Marion Square and enjoyed the walk down King Street to Walgreens. There were a good many young people at the counter, but they were able to find a booth and ordered sandwiches and Cokes. A couple of Citadel cadets came over and spoke. She remembered them from the dances she had gone to with Charlie that spring.

"You're the real queen bee," said Tee.

"When you go to a Citadel dance it's easy to be a queen. Those boys stay locked up during the week and any ole country girl looks good to them on Saturday night," she said, but without conviction.

"I know better than that," said her brother. "Those cadets have a good eye for girls — especially Charlie Rowland."

"Let's not talk about me, let's talk about you. Are you planning to be a monk?" Mary asked.

"I don't know much about monks, but from what little I do

know I don't think it's in my future. I just might break into the social world at any time. Major Manigault has asked me to go to his church with him and he says they have plenty of pretty Huguenot girls over there dying to meet a tarnished Presbyterian," he said facetiously.

"Who says you're tarnished? They'd better not say it in front of me. I'll tarnish their noses," she said, balling up her fist menacingly. "You're no criminal; you're a victim of some really bad luck and bad people."

"Well, big sister, I've been to jail and that's what people see, and I understand that. If Charlie had been to jail, he wouldn't be dating my sister without a whole lot of explaining. If I meet the right girl I'll do all the explaining necessary to satisfy those who care about her, but I haven't met one yet and I still have a lot to do…like helping get the farm back and marrying off my ugly duckling sister."

She looked fondly across the table at her brother and again rolled up her fist and shook it at him jovially. They continued to chat about this and that until they finished their lunch. They were preparing to leave when Mary's face took on a serious look and she asked, "Tee, are you doing something unlawful?"

"I'm not doing anything to hurt anyone. If you're referring to Jake Burton and his hoods, I'm only protecting myself and letting them know that I know how to balance the books," he replied.

"Did you break into his place?"

"I've been over that with the police and my probation officer. Don't make me defend myself to you."

"I'm sorry," she said. "I just don't understand your rules."

"Well," said Tee, "I don't understand everyone else's. There are those I trust and those I don't trust and the ones I trust aren't many."

Mary studied his face a while and then they got up to leave. She put the conversation back on the original happy track and they held hands strolling back to Chapel Street. She was aware that their worlds were different now and she had to trust the men in her life. Her daddy was back on course, Charlie was never off course, and Tee was out there somewhere doing things she didn't understand.

Perhaps I need to be a better Presbyterian, she thought.

As they turned down Chapel Street a little boy was turning a jump rope which was tied to a power pole. His big sister was jumping and singing:

Last night...the night before...

A lemon and a pickle came knocking at my door...

I went upstairs to get my gun...

You ortta seen the lemon and the pickle run!

This brought a wide grin to Tee's face and he and Mary looked at each other and laughed.

Chapter 27

Meeting the Parents

Because of Charlie Rowland, Mary had been introduced that spring to a new world. Charlie was popular at school and was from a well-established Charleston family. As a senior at The Citadel, he was proud to introduce his "queen," who surprised him as well as everyone else by her ability to move into his circle of friends with such ease and confidence.

At the first dance she attended, she wowed them all with her natural beauty and charm. In addition, she could do all the dances well, including the Charleston, because of her Saturday practices with her girlfriends at Mrs. Timmons's boardinghouse. Charlie was proud, but not a little bit aggravated by a couple of guys who were more attentive than he thought they should be. Mary noticed and called him silly, which didn't help. What did help, though, was that every time a dance ended, she came looking for him and was courteous to the other cadets but not encouraging.

On an evening when they were to attend a dance at the Yacht Club, Mary agreed to have Charlie pick her up early and take her by his parents' home for cocktails. Charlie also invited Tee, who declined. There was nothing spectacular about the family and they were happy to have it that way. "Substantial" would be the best word to describe them, but they were a lot more than that. They liked each other and had fun in their home. They were secure in many ways: financially, socially and in all of the ways families and homes are measured.

Charles M. Rowland Sr. was a respected banker, as was his father before him. It was expected that Charlie would follow this tradition, but the Rowlands weren't always sure about him. Never rebellious but not altogether compliant, Charlie seemed to hear a different drummer and march to it. That's one reason the family was not overly surprised to learn that he was dating a young lady he had met at the cigar factory. They were not overjoyed about it.

His brother, Michael, a high school sophomore, joked that she could roll some of those El Roi Tans for his daddy, who enjoyed a good cigar after dinner. He wasn't driven from the dinner table for this comment, but his mother fixed a gaze on him that he recognized as serious and intended to put an end to what she called "frivolous" conversation. His daddy laughed and broke the tension. They didn't know what to expect from this girl with the strange background who had so completely captivated their ordinarily very level-headed son. She had done it so quickly that Michael said that she had cast a spell over his brother. The wait was over when they heard Charlie enter the front door and announce his presence.

Mary was still casting spells, especially over Michael, who found himself speechless when she walked over to him as Charlie introduced her. She smiled as she took his hand; it was one down and two to go. Mr. Rowland was also easy, but mothers never are, so the critique went far beyond the blue eyes and big, genuine smile as Catherine Rowland took her turn meeting the object of her son's affections. After the preliminaries they were seated while

Mr. Rowland took drink orders. Mary followed the lead of her hostess and requested white wine. The men had Scotch and water and Michael reluctantly settled for a Coke.

"So," said Mr. Rowland opening the conversation, "Charlie says that you're in the tobacco business."

"Charles," said Mrs. Rowland sternly, "there's a lot more to talk about than business." Turning to Mary she said, "Business is all that matters to Charles…well, maybe golf too," she added, trying to take the conversation away from what she thought would be a source of embarrassment to their guest.

"I like to talk about business," replied Mary. "I don't know a lot about business but that's just one of the many things I don't know a lot about. I'm enrolling at the College of Charleston in September and business is one of the things I'm most interested in." She was looking at her hostess as she spoke. She then turned to her host and added pleasantly, "I work in tobacco. It's temporary but that's what I do. It's also what my family has always done; we planted it, raised it, cured it, and ultimately sold it to people like the ones I work for now. It's really interesting; it's unpleasant to work in until you get used to it, but after you get accustomed to the odor it's not bad and it's a good money crop."

"Sort of like Charleston," said Charlie. "Once you get used to the odors you really love the place." They all laughed; the ice was broken.

After refreshments they chatted for a while and Michael, who had sat next to her all evening, offered to show her his baseball cards.

"Quit being so pushy, Michael," said his mother and instead invited Mary to look around the house and showed her some of the furniture and paintings she had collected. She was warmed by the genuine appreciation for these nice things shown by the young and inexperienced girl.

Charlie announced that it was time for them to leave and, after more handshaking and cordial conversation, the young couple left holding hands and descended the front steps with the athletic grace that only the young have.

"I like her," said Michael.

"That's an understatement," said his father. "So, you wanted to show her your baseball card collection, huh? Your brother won't put up with such obvious flirtation for long."

"She's special," said Mrs. Rowland. "Such a pretty person, gracious and warm. You know what I liked best about her?"

"What?" asked her husband?

"Her rough hands with the tobacco stains; she made no attempt to either conceal them or to explain them. She's genuine and honest and I'm proud of our son's choice."

* * * * *

It was after one o'clock when Charlie came home and headed for the kitchen, where he saw a light.

"What are you doing prowling around in the kitchen at this hour?" he asked his mother, who was sitting at the table eating a cookie and drinking a glass of milk.

"You know full well what I'm doing. I'm waiting for you."

"You don't usually wait up for me. What's on your mind?" he asked with a grin.

"I want to talk about you and Mary McLauren. She's precious and we all like her — especially Michael, who I believe sees you as competition. Are you serious about her?"

"More than I can tell you. I know that I want to marry her and keep her with me as long as I live," he answered, surprised at his openness.

"I think you need to know her longer. You shouldn't rush into a marriage, even to someone as nice as Mary. You've got your military obligation and God knows what all before you. Take your time; she'll wait if she loves you. Have you asked her?"

"You don't have to worry about that. Yes, I've asked her, and she said no. Oh, she was nice about it, but it was a definite no."

"She turned you down. Well. Who does she think she is?" his mother demanded indignantly.

"Ha ha ha!" laughed Charlie. "She's the lovely girl you liked so much and who you said would wait if she loved me. She said she would and simply wants to go to the College of Charleston first. I'm OK with that. Like you said, I have a lot of things before me. Good night, Mother," he said, kissing her on the cheek, and went to his room pleased with everything.

Catherine Rowland looked at her watch and noted that it was 1:30 a.m. and she would have to wait another six hours before she could call Cousin Charlotte.

Chapter 28

Another Evening at Mannie's

Mannie and Frank Manigault were settled in the leather furniture, sipping good Scotch whiskey, and giving no indication that they were eager to get to the cooking chores. They planned steaks and potatoes and the Major was the chef du jour. The Scotch was a present from one of the Major's customers and he and Mannie had been sipping along on it for the last two cookouts, a little at a time. It was good sipping liquor, and they were enjoying it neat the way good Scotch should be treated.

"Have you seen or heard from Tee?" asked Mannie.

The Major shook his head and said, "Detective Tillman called me the other day, so I went by his office. He told me that he was pretty convinced that Tee was the one who took the money from Burton. That's twice now and he won't tolerate that kind of behavior from anyone. It's not just a matter of protecting Burton, he said, he just couldn't condone what he sees as a major crime. He told me that he had warned Tee and was watching both of them, Burton and Tee. He knows Burton and what he is capable of doing so he's really protecting them from each other." The serious look on the Major's face replaced what had been a relaxed and happy expression.

"Do you think Tee robbed Burton?" Mannie asked.

"I'll tell you I do, and I know that you think so too. I've gone out on a limb for Tee and won't go out any further. He's living close to the edge and isn't experienced or smart enough to get away with it. I'd hate it, but I won't be surprised to see him back on the train to Florence before this year is up," said the Major.

He got up from the sofa and strolled over to the kitchen area and inspected the potatoes and steaks. Mannie had already tossed up a salad which was on ice in the box and the coffee was perking on the stove.

The Major sat down at the table to peel potatoes and Mannie joined him as they continued the conversation.

"Tillman is right. We have to live by the rules we have, and nobody has a right to write the law to suit them," Mannie said thoughtfully. "We've both spoken to Tee and we know he understands all of this. It's a stubbornness he has that makes him go after Burton or anyone else who does something to him or his family. Everyone says what a good boy he was before the accident that took his mother and, really, took his father too. No one has seen any tears in his eyes since the night his mother died; it's like he was shocked into becoming another person. He's a tough young man and apparently willing to go back to prison if he has to but he isn't going to back away from Burton and his crew."

"Well, it looks like we'll all get caught up in this war pretty soon anyway. Maybe he'll get called into the Army and get away from all of this," the Major mused. "He'd make a good soldier. If he really did climb down into Burton's and then climb back out, he has outstanding courage and physical ability. Think about it; it would take a lot of moxie to do what he did to Burton, assuming, of course, that he did it."

The two men finished peeling and slicing the potatoes and the Major seasoned and broiled the steaks. A little wine with the meal, followed by strong black coffee and an El Roi Tan cigar, possibly rolled by the pretty hands of Mary McLauren, and the mood changed back to less serious concerns before the Major made his departure.

He walked back up the alley to his car, which was parked in the middle of Chapel Street and drove home thinking about Tee and the mystery of the boy. *He's too young for the activity he's involved in: breaking and entering, major theft, physical confrontations with really mean men*, he thought. He couldn't help but compare what Tee was doing with the kind of things he had done at that age. He also couldn't help but think about the things the boy wasn't doing: playing ball, chasing girls, hanging out at the soda fountain. He looked like a boy and often sounded like one, but he definitely wasn't one. He was truly unique.

When the Major had departed, Mannie poured another cup of coffee and seated himself back on the big, comfortable sofa and let his mind drift. He hadn't been sleeping well lately and knew that this additional cup of coffee wouldn't help him solve that problem. *I just hope that boy sees the light and changes before he gets hurt again*, he thought.

Chapter 29

The Interview Continues

The reporter strolled down the alley and greeted the animals before getting back to his interview with Mannie. He patted the dog, stroked the horse, and even held the cat on his lap briefly before the purring was over and she brushed him off. "Do you think Tee wanted to go back to the farm or do you think he had adjusted to city life and preferred to stay in Charleston?" the reporter asked Mannie.

"I don't know. He learned his way around the city and proved that he could make money and that he could protect himself. He definitely wanted to pay for the farm and for the family to have it back, but whether or not he wanted to live there, I don't know," Mannie replied. "It would be hard to say that he had adjusted to the city too. The things he did all related to making money to do what he wanted to do, but he had no social life to speak of, he didn't even have dress-up clothes."

"So, his daddy was at sea and Mary was working and being courted by Charlie Rowland, so she was also being drawn away from Tee. It seems unnatural for a boy his age to have no more social interest than he had," the reporter observed.

"Well, his work and business took a lot of time and he could never really relax because he knew that Burton and his people would love to get their revenge," said Mannie.

"What did he do to protect himself?"

Mannie replied, "He stayed off their turf for one thing. He was smart enough to know that the odds were in his favor around Chapel and Judith Streets. Burton's people would be noticeable if they lurked around where Tee lived and had friends."

"Did they ever come after Mary?"

"She was pretty much protected; Essie was with her going to and coming from work and she didn't go places alone. They wanted Tee but he was cautious. There wasn't a lot going on during that time. Charlie had graduated and Mary spent her weekends with him, attending parades and dances until he had to report for active duty. He went with the Army Air Corps and ended up in flight school at Shaw Field in Sumter. He could come home frequently, and Mary liked to visit him there because that was close to home for her."

"What about Tee, what was he doing during that summer?"

"He and Leon were doing well with their business. Leon opened the store on Saturdays when he didn't have to work at the docks. When he couldn't open it himself, either his sister or Tee would be there, and their business was doing well, especially the lending part. Their capital base was growing so they could lend more. They also continued to sell their rowboats and other marine stuff.

"Because he was so thrifty Tee was accumulating money. He did buy a suit to wear when he went with Mary to some of her social affairs, but that was rare. He charged the suit at Needle Brothers, who outfitted him with all the accessories. Mary was really proud to see her brother so well dressed and, to her, so handsome. He was always courteous when she introduced him around, but he didn't get too involved in conversation with others. It wasn't long before they stamped him as peculiar and allowed him to stand off and observe. Several young women cast inviting glances in his direction, but he would smile and look off. At first they were puzzled, then irritated, and then they looked elsewhere."

Mannie supplied this information quietly and thoughtfully while he sipped his coffee and looked away from the reporter, and then he added, "And of course, there was a war coming on."

Chapter 30

Pearl Harbor

It was eight o'clock on a Sunday morning in Pearl Harbor, Hawaii, where people were entering what they thought would be another routine day of rest with minimal work or stress. The first bombs struck the airfield at Oahu, then struck over the harbor where a large portion of the American Pacific fleet was anchored. The *U.S.S. Arizona* was one of the targets and when her powder magazine exploded, a thousand American sailors died on that ship alone. The second wave came at 8:30 and damaged 21 ships and 300 warplanes with a death total of 2,400 and 1,178 wounded. It was a sneak attack that took place while the envoys from Japan were engaged in peace negotiations with their counterparts in Washington.

When the news reached the rest of the nation later that day, the reaction was quick and decisive. The people were united in rage. The next day, President Franklin D. Roosevelt went before Congress, which resulted in a declaration of war. He addressed the people by national radio broadcast, declaring that December 7, 1941, was "a date which will live in infamy."

Never before or since has the nation been more united in a feeling of patriotism. In Charleston, Mr. Thompson was viewed in a new light and so were the Japanese, who had won a startling victory. But the sleeping giant was awake.

WINTER 1941–42

Chapter 31

War Changes Everything

The news was a shock to everyone. Mannie was leaving church, the Major was seated with his family at the dinner table, Mary was having dinner with Charlie's family, and Miss Charlotte had just gotten home from church. No one knew for certain where Tee was at the time and no one saw him for several days.

On the afternoon of the following day the Major came down the alley and he and Mannie talked. It turned out that Mr. Thompson wasn't the only one with an eye on the Japanese and the Major had contacts with people in Washington whose job it was to do just that.

"Of course, it's a surprise," said the Major, "but the surprise was that it could be done so secretly and so successfully. It was well-known that the Japanese resented the American presence in the Pacific and that they believed that Asia was for Asians, but the attack and its timing was the surprise. The Japanese had invaded Manchuria in 1937 because they needed expansion from an island too small to sustain their population. They even had a name for it: manifest destiny. People in Washington knew about Admiral

Yamamoto and that he and his staff had a prepared strategy for such an event, but they thought it was a defensive strategy rather than offensive."

Their conversation extended over a wide area which included the American view of the Japanese as depicted by cartoonists that never took them seriously. That had changed.

Mary and Charlie viewed their future differently. Charlie wanted to get married immediately, which wasn't different from how he felt before, but Mary was determined to finish college first.

Miss Charlotte was consumed by fear because her son was stationed at Honolulu and she had not heard from him. She followed her usual practice of putting things out of her mind by engaging in work and activities at church.

Tee was mostly out of sight while making big changes in his life. He cashed in his investment in the business with Leon and opened a bank account in which Leon would deposit the balance of the money as it became available. He took Mary to lunch at Walgreens and told her about the bank account, which was in his name and hers, and arranged for her to go to the bank and sign the account card. The account was for her education and she could pay him back when it was his turn, but his immediate future was with the U.S. Marine Corps. He told her that he had already signed up and would be going to Parris Island in five days. She consented to accept the money after strenuous objections but agreed on the condition that she would pay it back. The conversation was quiet and serious as it had to be.

It was a few days later when a Western Union messenger turned his bicycle from Alexander Street onto Judith Street and leaned it against the steps of the home of Miss Charlotte. It was usually bad news when a telegram arrived and this one was from Washington. He rang the bell and Miss Charlotte came to the door and knew immediately. She took the telegram and stumbled to her wicker chair and sat trembling with her eyes shut and the message unopened. It was two hours later when Mary and Essie found her still seated there. Essie stayed with her while Mary went inside and called the Rowlands. She then went into the kitchen to prepare for the arrival of the family.

Shock and grief. The shock stuns the body and the grief invades the heart with an all-consuming sadness that wounds and scars the soul.

It was Saturday morning when Tee arrived. He had waited until he knew that Miss Charlotte would be alone. She was sweeping the porch and put the broom aside and invited him to take a seat in one of the wicker chairs while she took the other. They sat in silence for a short while, then Tee stood and faced her with his head and eyes down. "You have been so good to so many people and you are the one to suffer. I've been so self-centered and dishonest with you and many others and it pains me to see you suffer. I've taken from you. I took things from your garage and convinced myself that it was alright because you didn't use them and wouldn't miss them. I thought I could do a few things for you and it would balance out. I was wrong. I've wronged you and others, and I feel great shame. I want your forgiveness before I leave."

"Where are you going?"

"I leave for Parris Island Wednesday. I joined the Marine Corps Monday afternoon and have been putting things in order. Apologizing to you is the most important thing I need to do."

"I knew about those things, Tee," she replied. "Things mean very little as we get old. They are expendable and can be replaced, but you are not expendable and cannot be replaced. I lost my son. Many others will lose theirs before this thing ends and you are so young and just starting out in life. I want you to come home. I'll pray for you every day and see you as a part of my life. Remember me. Write to me and I want to write to you."

They stood up. She took his hand as he turned to leave and put her arms around his waist. Nothing more was said, and she sat down again when he left the porch.

It was a different young man who reentered Judith Street. Atonement and forgiveness have strength over sadness and depression. War changes everything…even a headstrong and independent young man who wiped his eyes as he walked back to Chapel Street.

Chapter 32

The Drill Instructor

It takes a special man to be a drill instructor, or DI. He must be a lot of things, but principally, the thing he must be is a dedicated soldier. The "boot" under his command has no options other than to do what he is ordered to do even, which is often the case, things that make no sense and which infuriate him. Sometimes he may be standing at attention on top of a footlocker reciting out loud that he's too stupid to be a Marine. For failing to wash his clothes to the satisfaction of the DI, he may stand at attention with a dirty sock under his nose while reciting something derogatory about himself or his ancestry. The DI could choose other less demanding duty, but he wants to be a drill instructor. The boot is in the field or doing some onerous chore but he's not out there alone: the DI is right there yelling and directing the entire thing.

Sgt. John Morgan wanted the job and was good at it. A professional Marine, he had served in China and was still a young man.

Tee was amused as he and 63 other men marched with

galvanized water buckets over their heads while the DI marched smartly alongside with his swagger stick under his arm, barking out commands.

"One Hup Areet Hup Areet Hup Areet ...In cadence count."

"One two three four, one two three four, one two three four," came the muffled response of the boots from under the buckets.

"I don't hear you," yelled the DI, taking the swagger stick from under his arm and pounding on the buckets like the men were some giant mobile xylophone.

Tee formed mental pictures of the scene and smiled. He was taller than most, so he marched at the head of the platoon, which meant he received a lot less attention than the "feather merchants" who brought up the rear. *Semper fidelis*, he thought to himself: "Always faithful."

The days passed and the platoon got better. After a week they felt like old salts and would call out, "You'll be sorry!" to the busloads of newcomers — just like the others had done to their group when they first arrived.

Tee said to his bunkmate Joe on the first day they arrived and were greeted with the "You'll be sorry" call, "Those guys just got here yesterday and already they're asserting their rank over us."

"Yeah," said Joe, "their uniforms are still stiff and shiny. They've got twenty-four hours of seniority over us." And they laughed.

The day before they had arrived at Yemassee, South Carolina, a place not known to many people, but all East Coast Marines know exactly where it is and remember their arrival there. The Marine Corps Receiving Station is a nondescript barracks with no frills and the place where the new recruits are welcomed by a tough and unsmiling sergeant.

"All right, you clowns…double time. Line up here and shut up. I'll do the talking and your job is to listen and do what you're told. You see this emblem, this globe and eagle? Anyone wearing it is your mama, daddy and preacher. You stand at attention when you're spoken to and listen. You do what you're told, and you'll be allowed to live and if you don't, you won't want to."

From Yemassee they were loaded on a truck and crossed the river into the Marine Corps Recruit Depot for the eastern United States, called Parris Island. They would be broken down and dismantled then put back together as new men. *Semper fidelis.* Always faithful. It is the thing that binds all Marines together and which enables them to move and fight as a unit.

Tee was ready for anything they offered. He smiled as the barber asked him how he wanted his haircut; he knew that the clipper was set on skin and whatever hair he had would be on the floor when he left the chair. He was right.

Next was stripping down and moving quickly through a shower, then a dusting down process designed to remove any body vermin, followed by a fast hustle through the quartermaster's warehouse, where he was on the receiving end of fatigues and boots tossed in his direction. Amazingly, they fit.

It didn't take long to get into the spirit of it. Marching, marching and more marching to a cadence sung out by the drill instructor, and they came together quickly as a unit marching in step. There's a satisfaction in stepping out at 120 per minute. Tee felt right at home and came to enjoy the barracks chatter, although he never participated. He was a part of the group but never a part of the conversation, except when he would talk quietly with one or another of the guys. He liked them and they liked him, but Tee was still different. He met guys from other parts of the country, which was new for him, but as he studied them, he saw how much they were alike except the way they talked and some of the things they talked about. Mostly things like food and entertainment. There was plenty of room for friendship as they were molded into Marines. He talked often with Henry, who occupied the bunk under his.

Sgt. Morgan taught them everything they knew up to this point. When the rifle was issued it was packed in grease and it was expected to be cleaned and kept that way, regardless of the weather or conditions. They learned that every Marine is a rifleman first and foremost. The commandant, pilots, cooks and bakers — all were riflemen before they became other things. If you dropped the weapon you would sleep with it; it became a part of who and what you were. Every rifle had a number that they were expected to remember, just like every Marine had a serial number that was as important as their name.

The rifle was carried on the right shoulder most of the time and would be moved smartly from one position to another according to the commands barked out and this was done with snap and a military sound. When being inspected, the Marine would present the weapon at port arms position with the bolt open, ready for the DI to snatch it with style and make the inspection. One day Tee had his weapon ready for inspection and Sgt. Morgan took it. While going through the inspection he looked intently at the rifle number stamped on the chamber. He then did a thing DIs like to do: he asked for Tee's serial number. It always worked. The boot would do as Tee did: he gave the rifle number. Then he was asked to give his serial number. Tee was aware of his mistake by now but gave his serial number. The usual comments followed whereby the DI expressed his surprise that the boot would have the same serial number as his rifle number. The boot simply stood at attention and endured the embarrassment. It still wasn't over.

"Did your mother have any children who lived"? DIs liked to ask this question.

Tee didn't attempt an answer, but his eyes flashed immediate anger and his jaw moved as he struggled with his temper. Sgt. Morgan studied his face for a moment then moved on. He knew that he had seen something else in this recruit that set him apart.

Drill instructors don't establish friendships with boots and rarely have private conversations with them. It was after chow when they were all strolling back to the barracks that Sgt. Morgan came alongside Tee and quietly said, "My comment about your mother angered you and I apologize for that. You're a good boot and I'm proud of your progress. Let's forget it and move on."

"You're right, sir. My mother died three years ago, and it was painful. I protect her memory. You had no way of knowing and I appreciate what you are doing now, which I know is out of the ordinary. Thank you for that."

They weren't friends but a mutual respect was established.

Several weeks later the company moved to the range where they were introduced to the use of their rifles. Every Marine being a rifleman, they know that they can and will be called upon to fight with it. All are expected to qualify but those who qualify as expert are noticed and this ranks high in the eyes of their superiors. Marksmanship, physical endurance and leadership qualities — Tee demonstrated them all. This would be valuable when he later found himself in the First Marine Division and using the weapon up close.

The first lesson is called "snapping in" and it is an introduction to firing the weapon. From the prone position the shooter takes aim at a miniature target while his partner repositions the bolt by striking it back into place after the shooter simulates firing by squeezing the trigger and clicking the mechanism. From here he moves to the firing line and orients the weapon by moving the windage knob to move the sight from left or right toward the center of the target and the elevation knob to move the sight up or down.

Each shooter is allowed several rounds to accomplish this and is then ready to fire for the record. He fires from the prone, sitting and standing positions and the targets are raised with markers showing the spot where the round struck the target. A total miss is indicated by the embarrassment of a red flag — known as "Maggie's Drawers" — being waved across the target frame. It doesn't go unnoticed. This is important stuff and generates a lot of conversation in the barracks.

Basic training was drawing to an end and the DI had a softer tone in his voice and was even seen to smile on occasion… but not much. Each man knew he was still a boot and the DI was a Marine. Their hair was growing back, and some could even part theirs. The fatigues were soft and comfortable from wear and wash and the boots had molded to the feet. There was very little resemblance between the casual and undisciplined recruits and the sunburned and hardened young men who now marched as one and felt a unity and loyalty to the platoon — and the DI.

A strange thing was happening: The man who had made their lives miserable for weeks was being seen in a new light. Respect — one of the things we can't live without — was now appearing on both sides. The DI was proud of what he saw, and the new Marines were proud of what they had become.

How was this expressed? There's an unspoken tradition where an envelope is passed around and each new Marine puts a few dollars out of his first monetary payment in it and the envelope is placed under the sergeant's pillow. The gift is voluntary but is given with real affection. *Semper fidelis.*

There was a graduation parade with the post band playing and

the platoons marching before a reviewing stand with high-rank-
ing brass and noncommissioned officers looking with pride on the
trooping and stomping of the strong and impressive young men
they had trained. No longer boots, they wore the globe and eagle
and were ready to join the fight soon to be launched against the
Japanese who had killed so many Americans and destroyed so
many ships and installations. Tee felt the pride that comes with
being an American Marine.

Back at the barracks, they packed up their gear and prepared
for their ten-day leave while engaging in a lot of hand shaking
and backslapping with their buddies. Sgt. Morgan motioned to
Tee to step outside and told him that the platoon was shipping out
to Camp Lejeune at New River in North Carolina, where they
were forming the First Marine Division. He added that he was
going there too and invited Tee to join him for a beer at the Slop
Shute before leaving for Charleston. It was an honor for the new
Marine, and he accepted gladly.

"I don't drink but would enjoy trying a beer," said Tee.

"One won't hurt you and you will enjoy listening to the bull
being tossed around," the sergeant said. "I will get you to Yemassee
for a later bus to Charleston."

The afternoon at the Shute was fun. A lot of talk about a
lot of past experiences was shared by the old guys and the glass
of beer was good. Tee stopped at one beer, and it was getting
dark when he arrived at Yemassee to wait for the Jacksonville bus,
which was late, and this would cause him to arrive at Charleston
late at night. That too didn't matter.

Chapter 33

On Leave

The bus unloaded at the Charleston bus station at eleven o'clock that evening. There was a cold rain falling as Tee stepped out and headed to Anson Street. Rain dripped down his neck and into his collar, but the young Marine seemed not to notice. He shifted his seabag to his right shoulder and hit a good stride of 120 steps per minute and was soon turning off Calhoun Street onto Elizabeth and then to Chapel Street.

Once on Chapel Street, Tee walked in the middle of the wet and slick cobblestones, as was his practice, until he entered the alleyway leading to the warm and friendly hay bales of Mannie Simmons's home and stable.

A friendly grunt from Mannie's big dog was rewarded with welcome strokes on his head and back, and Tee found what he wanted most: dry and warm hay bales. A quick change of clothes ushered him into a deep and happy sleep. He awoke to the aroma of fried bacon and once again looked into the face of his good friend, who was preparing the homecoming breakfast.

"Get out here and wrap yourself around a Mannie Simmons breakfast," he said. "The Major is on the way and we have some catching up to do."

It was just a few minutes before the Major came down the alley. Tee noticed there was a little more shuffle to his stride than before, but he still wore the contagious grin that radiated friendship.

"Well, at last he's home again," Frank Manigault said. "Mannie, does the new Marine look very much like the ex-con did with a biscuit in his cheeks?"

"Come to think of it, he does," Mannie responded. "I think it's the way he grins around the biscuit. Total dedication. That's what it is. Let's see what he learned at Parris Island."

The Major's face turned more serious. "It's great to see you again, son," he said to Tee. "You've added another dimension to your education and none of it has been gentle or academic. Where you're going, the things you know will help you a lot more than poetry or philosophy. I envy you and wish I could go with you."

"You will go with me," Tee said sincerely, "you and Mannie and others who have been kind and helpful to this hard-headed ex-con who had the good fortune to stumble into a good place and find good friends. You were with me at Parris Island and occupied my thoughts and are a part of my extended family. I know what I'm headed out to do and I'm learning how to do it, but I don't know why and how it all came about."

"Most people don't," the Major said, "and they never do. I have friends who keep me updated and the more I learn, the more I know that history repeats itself." He inhaled the fragrant breakfast and said, "Let's do justice to Mannie's cooking before we go to war."

Reunions are mostly pleasant occasions and even more so when it is known that they are very temporary and may be the last. The conversation was lively, and a lot of old times were re-lived. After a long silence, the Major spoke.

"One of the lessons to be learned from this is that when faced with an enemy you must assume that he is set on doing harm to you," he said. "In preparation it's important to know three things: who, when and how. We knew that the Japanese were our enemy, but we went to sleep on the other two things. The failure to know the when and how represents a monumental failure on the part of our intelligence people and the cost is very high. We will win the war, but it will cost us a lot in money and lives. It already has."

"I don't understand how we came to be enemies with Japan," Tee said. "They are half a world away from us; I don't even know a single Japanese person."

"They live on a small island that doesn't provide enough resources to sustain them," the Major said. "That's why they invaded Manchuria in 1937. They have been led to believe that they can conquer the world since their alliance with Italy and Germany. They call themselves 'the Axis Powers' and share the same vision Adolf Hitler does — world domination. They call it manifest destiny, the same phrase used by us to justify what we did to the American Indians."

"I guess it's best sometimes not to know too much," Tee admitted. "I know that the Japanese killed Americans and threaten our country and that's enough for me. I like the Marine Corps and the slogan *semper fidelis*. I know that the Marine next to me when the day ends will be there when the sun comes up again… dead or alive. I'll do the same."

"It's a great slogan, always faithful. The Coast Guard has one I like a lot too, *semper parades*…'Always prepared,'" said the Major. "The Japanese will regret attacking our country." He looked at Tee with fondness. "We'll need to finish this conversation before you leave, but you have a few days to rest and reunite with a lot of others. We'll get together before you go."

Tee felt the warmth of the two men who had been in his corner from the start and was surprised that they would care for someone so different from themselves. *Maybe it's because they are so different from each other,* he thought … correctly.

Mannie said, "Miss Charlotte is planning a reception for you that includes your friends. The Major and I will be there. I know that you want to get out of here and go to the college and find Mary and we have held you up enough. Get going!"

Chapter 34

A Good Time with Friends and Family

For a Marine used to marching many miles a day, the walk from Chapel Street to the College of Charleston on a mild winter day was a pleasant stroll. Classes were in session when Tee arrived at the quadrangle. He seated himself on a bench in the big circle and studied the old buildings while he waited for his sister.

The academic setting was something new for the young man, who had so far found his education in different places. It pleased him that Mary was here and belonged here. She was smart and gentle with the kind of courage that would lead her to a world very different from the one of their shared past. Tee pondered briefly how, if ever, he would fit into Mary's world. A bell rang and these thoughts were replaced with a study of faces in the crowd until he found the one he was looking for.

"Tee! You're home!" she shouted gleefully as she raced over to her brother, who looked so different in his uniform. *No longer a boy but a man*, she thought, and then realized that he had been a man for a long time.

After a long and exuberant hug, she turned to a pretty brunette who had joined them. "Meet my friend," she said. "This is Elizabeth Masters. We have some classes together. We're both freshmen although I'm years older than her."

"Nonsense," replied Elizabeth. "You have a couple of years on me but I'm old for my age," she added, laughing, and looking into the eyes of Mary's brother. He noticed.

"Wait for us. We have one more class and we're through for the day," Mary said. "Elizabeth has her daddy's car and we can ride with her to pick him up at the shipyard."

"Great!" Tee said. When the girls headed to their class, he took a stroll around the small campus and then up Calhoun Street to the drugstore where he had a dish of ice cream, one of the things he loved most, and which he rarely had at Parris Island.

Tee got back just as the classes ended. The girls joined him, and they walked to the parking lot. They wedged together into the front seat of Elizabeth's father's car, a blue 1940 Chevrolet, with Mary in the middle, and headed north on Meeting Street. Tee noticed the "B" sticker on the windshield, which allowed slightly more of the rationed gasoline because the owner had an essential job.

"Does your father work in the shipyard?" Tee asked Elizabeth.

"Yes," she replied.

"What does he do?"

"He's a sort of supervisor," she said.

"There's been a lot of people move here to work there and they pay a lot more than most other local jobs," Tee said.

"We've been here a little over a year and like it a lot," Elizabeth replied. "Charleston is a great place with so much history and other things to see and do. We live on Rutledge Avenue close to the high school."

Tee said very little after that and looked out the window as they drove up Meeting Street. The girls talked about school and girl things. They arrived at the main gate, manned by a Marine guard, and were looking for a place to park when a Marine captain saluted the guard and walked toward the car. *A sort of supervisor!* thought Tee as it became clear the captain was coming to their car. Tee opened the door and he and Mary slid out as the captain approached the driver's side door. Tee snapped to attention and rendered a crisp salute.

"Just in time," the captain said as he slid into the driver's seat, which Elizabeth had vacated for the passenger's seat. She turned sideways so she could see both her father and the passengers now seated in the back.

"Dad, this is my good friend Mary McLauren and her brother Tee, who just finished boot camp at Parris Island," she said. "This is my father, Captain Phillip Masters."

"I figured Mary to be your school friend and I also figured that Tee had just finished Parris Island," said Captain Masters. Turning around in his seat, he continued, "It's nice to meet you both. Mary, Elizabeth has a lot to say about you and it's all good. We are pleased that she has you as a friend. And Tee, how did you like Parris Island?" he asked while looking in the rearview mirror as they drove off.

"It was what I expected, sir, and I didn't have much trouble with any of it except when they wouldn't let me sleep," he said. "All that middle of the night stuff was difficult for me because I sleep soundly, and it was hard for me to jump out of my bunk and take everything outside and scrub the deck with bricks and sand." He paused, wondering if he had been too honest. "I liked most of it, sir, and understood what they were doing to us and why."

"Did it make you mad?" Captain Masters asked.

"Yes, sir, sometimes, but they didn't know it."

"Wise lad. Did it bother you that they called you 'lad'?"

"Not really, sir. There were a lot of things worse than that, but, as I said, I understood why they were doing it."

"When you were concealing your anger, did you pout your lips?" Captain Masters asked with a smile.

Mary answered for him. "Tee is good at masking his feelings and very hard to read."

"I can read him," Elizabeth said. "It shows in his eyes."

"I guess I'll have to wear dark glasses around you," said Tee and they all laughed.

"Watch Elizabeth, son," Captain Masters said. "She's clever and that's dangerous."

"Pretty and clever, sir," Tee said, "and I'm just a country boy. But I'm fast on my feet and know when to run." They all laughed again, but Elizabeth looked Tee straight in the eyes for such a long time that he began to feel uncomfortable.

"Do you know where you are going from here?" Captain Masters asked Tee.

"Yessir. To New River to the First Marine Division and then to the Pacific," he replied. "My drill instructor is going there too, and I hope I can serve with him. He's a good man and has taught me a lot."

"Excellent! Mary, where can I take you?" Captain Masters asked.

"Drive us to Judith Street, if you don't mind," said Mary. "We will enjoy some cake and iced tea with a very nice lady who loves us both."

"That's good, because she has invited me to your homecoming celebration Wednesday night so I'm glad to know where she lives," Elizabeth said.

When they arrived at Miss Charlotte's home, Captain Masters stopped the car and let them out. "It is a pleasure to meet both of you," he said. As he drove away with Elizabeth, his thoughts turned immediately to what Tee had told him about his assignment. First Marine Division and to the Pacific was exactly where Captain Phillip Masters had made application for two days ago. *A good-looking Marine, and I hope we have a lot of them coming on because we sure will need them and I sure want to be with them*, he thought.

"Elizabeth, I like your friends," he said. "Mary is just as you described her and is someone you can trust and learn from, but she can learn from you too. She's had experiences far beyond her years which you have not, but you have been to places she has not. You can educate each other." He paused. "But be careful with that boy. He's only going to be here a short time and he may not be coming back."

"I know, but I like him," Elizabeth responded. "He'll only be here a week, but it will be fun while he's here with us."

Chapter 35

Miss Charlotte's Reception

They started arriving right at five o'clock and the front porch got crowded in a hurry. Mary and Elizabeth joined in ushering the guests inside and serving iced tea and punch. Miss Charlotte greeted each of them warmly but showered most of her attention on Tee. It was a stand-and-munch kind of party with plenty of good food on the dining room table where each guest could serve himself. Mannie and Major Manigault walked over from Chapel Street, bringing some adult refreshment along for those with stronger tastes.

It was a diverse group and the only thing they had in common was their association with Tee. Some felt the usual concern for a young man heading toward combat, and some felt great relief at seeing him changed from a borderline criminal to a Marine patriot. Some felt both, and Mannie and the Major were among this number.

Elizabeth's father had dropped her off and told her to call when she wanted him to pick her up, but she told him she would get a ride home. It was a question of time before she had a brief conversation with Tee and her escort home was arranged. With this done, she went back to working the table and the kitchen with her friend Mary.

As it was a mild night, Major Manigault and Mannie set themselves up in a corner of the porch and were enjoying the company of the men who had a disdain for the tea and punch. About an hour into the reception, the Major called the crowd together for a toast.

"We have with us a young man for whom we all have developed a great affection and we honor him as a new member of our armed forces," he began. "Our country has been attacked and many of our young men have been killed in a sneak attack on our installations at Pearl Harbor and in the Pacific. Mistakes have been made that allowed this attack to catch us off guard, but the biggest mistake was made by the Japanese. Have no doubt, we will win this war. It will cost us dearly in many ways, and the most painful cost will be in the lives of Americans and their allies.

"Tee, you are now and will continue to be in our thoughts and prayers and we are proud of you and your commitment to our country. I hope the few days you have here will provide you with such memories that will find a place in your heart and mind as you join your fellow countrymen in reminding the Japanese and the rest of the world that Americans will fight for their country and the freedom we enjoy," he concluded.

There was a round of heartfelt applause. Everyone there felt a flush of patriotism and a togetherness that was new to them all. The party began to break up a little later and the ladies all tidied up the house and showed their appreciation to Miss Charlotte. Mary looked around for Elizabeth and determined that she had quietly left. She couldn't locate Tee either. She smiled and went home.

* * * * *

It was all new to Tee. Holding hands and strolling with a pretty girl released emotions he had never felt. The trauma of his losses and the dedication he had to replace them and his determination to get revenge against anyone who treated him unfairly were all-consuming and demanded strength and courage. Exchanging glances and holding hands with a pretty girl brought forth new feelings, and the otherwise strong and brave young man found himself puzzled and unsure of how to act or what to do. Not so with Elizabeth; she knew, and took charge.

The walk home took them to the soda shop at the Francis Marion Hotel where they slurped milkshakes and chatted. She asked questions and he gave guarded responses. When they arrived at her home on Rutledge Avenue, they sat on the porch a while until her mother came out and, after brief introductions, reminded Elizabeth that tomorrow was a school day. Tee left and Elizabeth joined a family meeting with her parents, where her father again cautioned her about her new friend.

"He's exactly what the Marine Corps wants. He wears the expert rifleman medal and he wears the uniform well. He obviously loves the Corps and shows respect for authority. However, you should know that he has been to prison for inflicting serious bodily harm on some pretty tough men," her father warned. "You're a young and vulnerable girl."

"I know how to be careful but in our relationship he's more vulnerable than I am. He's gentle and shy with me," Elizabeth replied. "He is paying his sister's way through college and is protective of her. His mother's memory is sacred to him and these have been the women in his life. You'll see because he will be coming here a lot while he's on leave. You should also know that he didn't come on to me...I drew him in."

"I know," said her father. "I saw it, and he was surprised but not more so than I was. I've never seen you so bold."

"I don't feel bold, I feel comfortable," Elizabeth protested. "Mary has told me a lot about her brother. He's unusual and I like him a lot, and he likes me. He knows his way around in a man's world, but he's out of his element socially and especially with women. I'm as safe with him as I would be in Sunday School."

They all laughed and decided to sleep on it and went to bed, each thinking over what they had just heard.

* * * * *

Tee stepped lively on the way back to Chapel Street and reflected on these new events in his life. Up until now he was focused on where he knew he was going and how he had to prepare himself to meet these challenges. This girl was not a part of his plan and, as much as he was attracted to her, he knew that next week he would be back on track. In the meantime, he liked her very much and would enjoy her company as much as he could.

Mary wanted to talk and was waiting up for him when he entered the apartment, but he avoided conversation and went straight to bed. She smiled to herself and went to bed knowing full well what the answers to her questions would be.

* * * * *

Mary was finishing a quick breakfast when Tee came in the next morning. "I smelled the coffee," he said, and poured himself a cup, picked up the *News and Courier*, and walked downstairs to sip and read on the front porch. She understood and rushed out of the house, but not before smiling at her brother and kissing him on the cheek. Tee quickly scanned the news and headed off to see Mannie, but first stopped by the grocery store for some eggs and bread — and was lucky enough to get some bacon.

Mannie was going through his chores when Tee arrived and put on the coffee and set about to help feed the animals. Breakfast followed and Mannie had questions.

"Tell me about her."

"What's to tell? She's Mary's friend and classmate and someone had to escort her home...so I did it."

"You're truly a nice guy. The prettier the girl the easier it is to be nice. It looked like you were on your best behavior," Mannie said with a grin.

"You like to pull a guy's leg, don't you? Quit dancing around and get to the questions I know you have. Major Manigault will need the answers too, so let's get on with it."

"OK. How did it go on your first date?"

"I walked her home where she lives with her father, a captain in the Marine Corps, and a man probably not too anxious to have his only daughter hanging out with a fuzzy recruit. I was cautious."

"Cautious? Ha. You were scared. Not as much of him as you were of her. You were also wise," Mannie said. "Pretty women can easily dominate a strong man, especially one who has never smelled the perfume up close. You'd better stay scared and cautious. It's easy to get carried away when they bat their eyes at you, but you don't want to leave her with a problem...and you know what I mean."

"Sure, I do," said Tee, slightly indignant. "In addition, she happens to be a captain's daughter and my sister's friend. I only want to have good memories when I leave, and a clear conscience. It's a new thing for me but I'm not stupid."

"There's a narrow line between foolish and stupid and none

of us is wise when it comes to women. You're a good man and need some eggs and bacon to set you straight," laughed Mannie. Tee knew a good Mannie Simmons breakfast and the quiet company of his friend would add another fine memory he could take with him

"It was a nice little party Miss Charlotte put on for you and your friends," Mannie said as he forked up eggs. "She really likes you, Tee, and sees you as a son. That's important to know. She has the gold star in her window and a vacancy in her heart. You should appreciate that and write to her when you go back."

"I know that and will write but I'm not too good at writing letters," Tee confessed. "She said a postcard is what she wants, and I have already bought some with the stamps already on them. I know your address too." He stood up. "I've got to go now, and I'll see you later. Do you need anything else from the store?"

"No. But hurry on; I don't want you to be late for class."

"You sure are funny sometimes," Tee said over his shoulder as he walked away, laughing.

* * * * *

Tee took his seat on the quadrangle as before and was just getting settled when the bell rang, and the girls appeared.

"Walgreens for lunch?" he asked. "It's on me."

"No arguments here," Mary said while Elizabeth nodded in agreement and they headed out. The little conversation on the walk was mostly between the girls and about the term paper they had to prepare for the next day. It was a short walk and they slid into the booth, the girls both on one side.

"No one wants to sit with me, I guess," Tee commented.

"No. We want to look at you. We want a picture of you in our mind and one for our mantelpiece," Mary said. "Is that OK with you?"

"OK with me, provided I get the same in return."

"It's a deal then, so let's study the menu," Mary said.

"Study all you want to but I'm giving the order. I've been ordered around for months now and today I'm giving the order."

"Where do you get the authority?" Elizabeth asked.

"I've been told that I have leadership potential and I'm ready to show it," Tee said with a grin. "As they say at the Island, 'Quiet in the ranks.'"

When the waitress arrived, the private with potential ordered with authority: "Three ham and cheese sandwiches and three vanilla milkshakes."

When their food was served, Elizabeth said, "I don't want to rush anyone, but I'll need to hurry off as soon as we finish. I have a term paper to do and we're having a dinner guest at home and I need to do some cooking."

"Is it anyone I know?" asked Mary.

"Yes," Elizabeth said, her eyes dancing with mischief. "Your brother."

"How do you know her brother will come?" asked Tee.

"He's ordered to. Ordered by the daughter of the captain, and their leadership qualities are well known. Seven o'clock," she added.

"I guess a 'yes ma'am' is in order and I guess I'll need to rush off too. I don't have to do a term paper, but I do need to go by the photo shop," Tee said. "You girls already have plenty of photos, I'm sure."

"One for the mantlepiece and one for the wallet — for each of us," Mary reminded him.

"Of course. Do I need to do my face?" he asked facetiously.

Chapter 36

Dinner at the Masters'

The doorbell rang exactly at seven o'clock and was answered by a man wearing a white shirt and a blue sleeveless sweater who invited Tee into the house while handing him a white sweater to wear.

"Slip out of that blouse and tie and put on this sweater so that we can talk man to man rather than captain to private," he said.

"Sure," said Tee while thinking to himself, *that might change my appearance but didn't exactly level the field.*

With the change the two men went into the den and were greeted by two women wearing aprons. "Welcome to our home," said Emily Masters, leading Tee to a very comfortable chair which was her favorite. The younger woman simply smiled brightly as they turned back toward the kitchen.

"This is a first. Elizabeth hasn't exposed any of her other friends to her cooking and I don't know if this works to your advantage or not," Captain Masters said. "She's usually content to leave that to her mother."

"Well," said Tee, "I eat what's put on the table and can't remember a time when I was asked to judge the meal. I can tell you now that I will like her cooking and let her know it. I'm flattered at being invited to your home and especially to be the first friend she cooked for. I'm also puzzled by her in many ways. You know that, of course."

"You're leaving in a few days which puts the relationship in a serious light, and I wanted to talk with you about my concerns," her father said. "She's young and much infatuated with you, which makes her vulnerable. I know that mistakes can be made at a time like this."

"I see that," said Tee. "You feel about your daughter and wife the way I feel about my sister. You are their protector, just like I am for my sister. I also care about Elizabeth in a way I've never felt before but I'm her protector also. Besides that, she's smarter than me and much more in control of things than I am. Maybe you should worry about your fellow Marine," he said with a broad smile that gave comfort to the concerned daddy. The bridge between a captain and a private began to narrow.

The women reappeared without the aprons and welcomed them into the dining room, where the table was set with the Masters' best china and silverware. "My!" exclaimed Captain Masters. "I would feel honored if I didn't know that I'm not the honored guest. Rank has its privileges but not always. Tee, I hope you realize that you have been elevated and I have been put in my place."

"No one questions your place, sir. You're the master of this house and I'm pleased to be welcomed here."

It was a good meal and all the things that needed to be said were said. Tee was relaxed and happy and joined in the lively conversation with ease and confidence…even with his superior. This is something else that would be remembered.

Emily came into the den where the men had again retired, followed closely by Elizabeth. "Tee, take my daughter downtown and buy her a dessert. Phillip is going on KP duty and has a choice: wash or dry. You are excused this time but when you come again you can join him, and I'll go for the dessert."

"Yes, ma'am," said the private, executing a snappy salute, and was slipping on his blouse and tie as they headed for the door.

"What a great meal and what a great family. If you intended to make my head swim you succeeded," Tee said to Elizabeth as they walked down the street. "It's a good thing I'm headed out of town because right now I'm lost in the woods. Where's the soda shop?"

"Down Calhoun Street. Don't worry. I'm not lost, and I will protect you from everyone and everything except me. Just do what I tell you and you'll be OK."

The bond was set. No plans could be made, and no vows would be taken but true affection was established, and they relaxed and enjoyed the pleasure of simply being together and doing nothing else that mattered. A strawberry sundae is a grand way to top off such an evening for two people just leaving their teen years and on their way to adult lives filled with serious challenges...especially Tee.

A happy stroll took them back to Rutledge Avenue where they said good night and Tee greatly enjoyed the fragrance of perfume up close before once again stepping lively on his way back to Chapel Street. Once again Mary was anxious for conversation and once again Tee led her in another direction.

"I've got some postcards already stamped and I'm going to address some of them so I can save time later and will only need to write my message," he said.

"That's a good idea and Elizabeth and I have already planned to do that for you, so put them down and let's visit a little."

Tee gave up. "Yes, to answer your unasked question, I like her a lot and you've talked with her enough to know about how she feels. You know a lot more than I do so let's talk about family. Have you heard from Daddy? Being at sea makes it hard for him to communicate with anyone but he should be coming home soon. I'll want some cards addressed to him and we can use your address."

"That's a good plan. What are your plans for tomorrow?"

"I don't want to become a fixture at the college, and I need to make some visits to other friends. I want to spend some time with Miss Charlotte and with Mannie and the Major too. Time is running short. I want to tell you now that I feel confident about where I'm going and what I will be doing. I also feel confident that I will come back fine, and we can all pick up our lives and move on. What I'm asking you to do is not worry too much about your brother, who is pretty good at taking care of himself. I'm not going to worry about you because you are on the right track and I'm proud of you just like always. Now, I'm sleepy and know exactly how to address that problem. Good night," he said as he kissed his sister and walked off.

Mary returned to finishing her term paper and then sat alone on the third-floor porch for a while, reflecting over the many changes in her life and feeling thankful for her good fortune. Purpose, she knew, was the only path to contentment and she knew hers and renewed her commitment to pursue it to the best of her ability. These thoughts were still on her mind when she turned off the light and lay her head on her pillow.

Chapter 37

Wrapping it Up

Friday morning early Tee was on the bus headed to Manning and a meeting with Cousin Henry, where he would sign off on some banking business and power of attorney giving Mary complete authority over all of his business. A brief meeting followed, then he was on a return bus to Charleston.

It was a little after one o'clock when he arrived at the dock for some farewells and then went to Miss Charlotte's for a private goodbye. Cake and tea were served as always, along with promises and the delivery of a small photo. There were no emotional displays, but serious promises were made. Then he walked over to Mannie's for the same purpose.

What do you say to such a friend who has been in your corner from the start? "Wise" and "kind" are just two things that could be said about Mannie and there are many more including "honest" and "loyal." Tee thought about how much Mannie had influenced his life and how he could never repay him.

Mannie was engaged in his usual routine of tending to

his animals and working in his small garden when Tee arrived. "Good to see you, Tee," he said and warmed him once again with his contagious smile. "You come and go, and it seems we never have enough time together. The Major and I would like to do something for you before you leave but anything we do would just be a duplication of what others have already done. Good friends don't need to be reminded, they remember and know that they're remembered. It's different now — very different, and dangerous. You're no stranger to danger but not immune to what can happen. Remember, you do have a lot of people pulling on the church bells for you."

"It's a lot different from when I first intruded into your home and life," Tee agreed. "I was a brash kid with my own ideas and not very receptive to what other people thought. You should have booted me off your property, but you didn't, and I can't begin to tell you how much I owe you and appreciate all that you have done for me. You and the Major quietly led me in a different direction, and Miss Charlotte reminded me of what I lost when my mother died. I told Mary last night that I am confident about where I'm going and what I will be doing and that I would make it back. I'm telling you the same thing and will need to find you here when I do. I plan to see the Major today and pay my respects to the fine gentleman that he is."

A cup of coffee and a warm handshake ended the visit and Mannie felt genuine emotion watching the now grown and strong Marine walk back to Chapel Street and into his dangerous future.

The visit to the Major was brief. There were many new organizations being formed for civilian support of the war effort and the Major was at the head of several of them. Mutual respect makes a strong bond and two men so different in background and temperament shook hands for the last time.

Packed and ready, Tee had made his rounds and said his goodbyes to his various friends. He had no trouble finding words with all of them but knew that the next one would be difficult. How much should he say? What could he expect from Elizabeth and what would she expect from him? War changes everything but they were both eighteen years old and faced with uncertain futures. He knew he would not tie her down and deny her a full college life, but he also knew that they loved each other. When he rang the doorbell on Rutledge Avenue, he was still uncertain.

"Come, in Tee," Captain Masters said, welcoming him into the den once again. "Elizabeth is powdering her nose and will be right down."

"Thank you, sir," Tee said taking his seat in the same comfortable chair as before. "You and Mrs. Masters have been very kind to a boot Marine who latched onto your wonderful daughter and was certainly not what you had planned. You have tried hard to make me feel at ease despite the obvious differences and I have appreciated your efforts. I've been very honored by this. Maybe we can serve together some time; it would be another honor."

The ladies came in and the conversation was changed but enough had been said. Captain Masters knew that there would be a lot of time for Elizabeth to reflect over things as she matured in college and in other ways.

"We've been invited to an evening of bridge but you two make yourselves some snacks and enjoy your evening," Mrs. Masters said. "Tee, it's been such a pleasure getting to know such a good Marine who has brought such pleasure to our house, especially to our beloved Elizabeth. We will remember you in our thoughts and prayers." This last was said with obvious emotion, and the parents soon waved good night and left.

Elizabeth led him into the kitchen where she put on some hot chocolate and sliced some apple pie. Tee joined her at the table and made short work of the pie. He sipped on the hot chocolate and talked about his good luck to have such a family and such friends, then he grew serious.

"You know I'll miss you," he told Elizabeth, holding her hand, "but you need to know that I won't allow you to make promises to me that will deny you the social benefits of college. If I were going to be here, I'd build a fence around you and stand guard over you with a shotgun, but I won't be here for a while. You know how I feel about you and you know that I'll think about you every day. I'll make this promise: I'll come home and, when I do, if I have competition, I'll be the strongest competitor anyone ever saw."

"I can declare the winner right now," Elizabeth said, her eyes filling with tears. "You get back and see."

They enjoyed being alone in the nice house until Tee said, "I've got to go now," and again he enjoyed the scent of perfume up close. Elizabeth handed him a small carry bag, which she said contained the postcards with her address on them. Tee thanked her and turned quickly and hurried away. Elizabeth stood at the door for a long while, then wiped her eyes and went inside.

The leave was over, and Tee had no desire for more farewells. After saying good night to Mary, he went straight to bed and long before daylight, he shouldered his seabag and quietly left. An hour later he was seated on the Jacksonville bus headed back to Yemassee and the things he had been training to do.

SUMMER 1942

Chapter 38

The Home Front

Among the things the war impacted was the friendship between Mannie and the Major. Major Manigault was consumed with the national effort to sell war bonds and finance the
great war machine it would take to defeat the Allies' enemies. The
social meetings on Chapel Street were mostly a thing of the past,
but Mannie would now go to the Manigault home and bring fresh
seafood and choice vegetables and leave them with the cook. It
concerned him that the Major was displaying serious physical
changes on the few occasions that they did meet; he looked old
and tired.

Mannie made a special trip to the Major's home on a Wednesday evening and they sat on the porch talking about the war. Tee
had mailed them each a postcard with very little information other than that he was at New River, North Carolina, and engaged
in serious training.

"The First Marine Division is working hard on perfecting
beach landings and new techniques never used in conventional

warfare," the Major said. "I hear things from my friends in Washington, but the information is scarce and guarded, as it should be. The attack on Pearl Harbor was devastating but not as completely destructive as the Japanese had hoped for. They're ambitious to control the South Pacific and the attack was designed to take out our fleet. They knew ahead that they could not win a long-term war with the United States but thought the attack would demoralize us, and we would withdraw. They were wrong and a lot of their top people know it." The Major displayed a lot of his old strength and determination as he recited these events but eased back down in his chair to regain his composure when he finished.

"Speaking of guarded, you need to be more careful about your health," Mannie said. "I don't need to tell you what your doctors have been telling you. You're pale and you have serious heart weaknesses. The things you are doing are important, but you won't be of much use if you don't slow down and pace yourself."

"I'm stronger than you think," said the Major.

"Not true, Mannie," said Mrs. Manigault, who was standing at the screen door. "You are a true friend and you are telling him what he needs to hear, but he's stubborn."

"Eavesdropping…my own wife snooping on her husband," said the Major, laughing as he winked at Mannie. "Bring that bottle of single malt from the den and bring a glass, dear," he said. "I can't drink right now but I can enjoy watching my friend have a glass." He shook his head. "Vicarious drinking! I never thought I would be reduced to that, but it will please me to see Mannie enjoy it. It evaporates, you know, and I hate to see it go to waste."

"It's never evaporated around this house; it disappears, but not from evaporation," his wife chuckled as she left to fetch the bottle and glass.

A few minutes later, Mannie had his glass of Scotch, which he sipped and sighed over with pleasure. "I've often been a consumer but never a performer, but maybe I can develop some talent along that line," he said with a lingering smile shared between the man he greatly admired and the wife who he knew shared his concerns. "I'm doing this for two reasons. First, I like the Scotch and then too I want to please my good friend. I won't perform again until you can join me, then we'll do it again. It's not much fun to drink alone. I'll see you again next week when I can locate some good shrimp or fish — maybe both."

"You can't leave before I return the favor and give you some advice. I'm not the only one pushing himself, and you had better slow down yourself," the Major said. "It's a great thing you are doing collecting scrap and junk with your wagon but neither you nor your horse are young. You need to pace yourself."

"It's fun to go around different neighborhoods where the kids are making their contribution by collecting it and we take it to Citadel Square where they pick it up," Mannie protested. "It's wonderful to see and to be a part of the total effort. You're in it and I am too. Did you know your war bond sales team now includes the paperboys? They sell war stamps that are pasted in little booklets until they add up to $18.75, then the boy takes it to the *News and Courier* and brings back a $25 war bond that matures in ten years. People are investing that have never invested before. Now they know that they can buy a bond at twenty-five cents a week and are impressed with how it earns interest. That's a new thing for them and it's good."

Mannie took another appreciated sip and regarded his old friend. "But that's enough about me. I repeat my message to you about backing off a little. A lot of people depend on you. There are enough casualties already. Mothers with sons in the service are putting blue stars in their windows and a lot of them are replacing them with gold stars. You and I can help, but only if we take care of ourselves. I for one want to welcome Tee back to Chapel Street and I want you to be there as before."

"Thank you, Mannie," said Mrs. Manigault while the Major nodded and smiled. "Incidentally, the Major and I want you to have that fancy carriage and harness outfit out back for two reasons: your friendship is the main one and the other is that you are the only person we know who can make good use of it. It's an old family thing we treasure and know that you will too."

Mannie was touched. "I don't know how to thank you. It's quite a price to pay for a few shrimps and a little seafood."

* * * * *

Back at Chapel Street Mannie gravitated between his horse and dog, giving each a special treat. Even the cat came down out of the stall and brushed against his legs and accepted some attention — on her own terms, of course.

Tee was training. Mary and Elizabeth were studying. Miss Charlotte was staying busy in her garden and had joined a club where the women knitted scarves for servicemen. She had a permanent lamp under her gold star. The war effort was underway and the country was united with such patriotism that would have struck terror into the hearts of America's enemies if they had seen it.

Chapter 39

First Marine Division

In May 1941, the First Marine Division had been divided between Quantico in Virginia and Parris Island in South Carolina, but very soon after that the men were aboard ship again for maneuvers off New River, North Carolina, where the Corps had bought 111,710 acres of water, swamp and coastal plain heavily infested with sandflies, ticks and snakes. Here they would practice and perfect beach landings and related amphibious training.

They lived in tents and were isolated from the outside world, and even the married officers were forced to stay on base except on weekends. The tents were set up on wooden platforms that had wide gaps between the boards and when winter came the men stuffed them with newspapers and magazines to keep the cold out. They practiced going over the side from ships and landing from small boats onto the beach.

On December 7, 1941, the regulars and reserves of the American armed services had been molded well but consisted of just 518 officers and 6,871 enlisted men. The war surprised almost all Americans, but not these; they knew that the purpose behind all that training was to fight a war and they expected it. Early in 1942 the Japanese had taken the island of Tulagi and in July they landed troops on Guadalcanal and began building an airfield. This would threaten the Allies' control of the New Hebrides and New Caledonia. The enemy had to be ejected.

As the Major had said, those who are charged with defense must know three things: who, how and when. The attack on Pearl Harbor had answered the first question. The United States had known that Japan was its serious enemy but utterly failed to know how and when the attack would come. Now the answers to all three were known to the United States, and it was Japan's turn to find these answers. The one who launches the attack only has two of the three questions to answer: when and how the target would fight back. The giant was awake and angry, and the Japanese were far from home and home was a very small place. They had taken control of much of the Pacific and now they had to defend what they had taken.

In May 1942, General Alexander Vandegrift and his First Marine Division were on board and the ships were headed toward the Panama Canal and to Wellington, New Zealand, where they docked on June 20 and began to move into hastily built quarters. Some used this spare time to write postcards and letters while most of the men introduced themselves to New Zealand girls. It had been a long time since they had liberty and they were welcomed by the girls, who found them to be generous and fun; the country's own young men were fighting in Africa.

General Vandegrift had been promised six months to train, and was informed that he now had one month to occupy and defend Tulagi and adjacent positions which included Guadalcanal. D-Day would be August 1 and it was a tribute to the general and the corps that they sailed from Wellington on July 22 to Koro Island in the Fijis for final training. They left Koro on July 31 for

Guadalcanal and the first American land offensive in the war. Among the men cleaning their weapons and sharpening their knives was a quiet and dedicated Tee McLauren.

Chapter 40

On the Offensive

It was a different kind of war. Amphibious warfare demanded that the sea and air be secure from enemy attack while the troops were being transported and vulnerable. The American Navy had suffered serious losses at Pearl Harbor and the remaining fleet was assembled like a pickup team that was facing an enemy team that had perfected its tactics with years of preparation and experience.

It was a different Marine Corps too. The hardcore old timers had been training for years and had established a tradition built around their motto, *semper fidelis*. Now the corps was swollen to more than twice its size with younger and different people. This only increased the hardened Marines' pride as they talked about the "Old Corps."

"I've worn out more seabags than you have socks, lad," was only one of the many expressions used to put the youngsters in their place. This would change when the shooting started, and the young ones proved themselves to be very worthy.

The convoy that steamed toward Guadalcanal represented most of the effective force the Navy had in the Pacific at that time. The *Saratoga, Enterprise*, and *Wasp* were the only available carriers and were escorted by the battleship *North Carolina*, some cruisers and several destroyers. The total strength of all the Marine units that embarked on the morning of August 7, 1942, was 956 officers and 18,146 enlisted men.

The convoy had the good fortune to travel under an overcast sky and was not challenged by Japanese air or surface forces. The men of the First Division, simply called "The First," began to go over the sides at 0647 hours (6:47 a.m. in civilian time) One man remembered them as "paled by days of inactivity, of being cooped up in the hold, dripping with perspiration." Their dungarees were wet with sweat and clung to their bodies as they went down the cargo nets. It was the beginning of the first American offensive against the Japanese in World War II.

The American public received the news with enthusiasm, remembering the attack on Pearl Harbor and the defeat in Corregidor. By then the Navy had won impressive battles at Coral Sea and Midway, but the Marines wanted to prove to themselves and their enemies that they could wield a rifle and a bayonet. There was a widespread belief that the Japanese were superior soldiers and that the Americans weren't as rugged. The events of the next four months settled that question as the foes came out of the jungle at one another day after day and met in hand-to-hand combat, grappling with knives and bayonets, and firing at one another with the small arms of the individual foot soldier. The end was always uncertain.

The first day on the island of Guadalcanal was easy. The Marines anticipated that they would be met on the beaches, the "stuff would hit the fan," they would have to fight to get ashore. Instead, nobody was hurt. First ashore were the First and Third Battalions of the Fifth Marines. The First Marines began to move at 1100 hours toward an objective known simply as "Grassy Knoll," which had appeared to be easily approachable from the inadequate maps available at that time. It turned out to be several miles away through thickest jungle. This was their introduction to the hellhole known as Guadalcanal.

At 12:30 p.m. a force of two enemy engine bombers struck at the convoy. They sank nothing and damaged only one destroyer, but it halted the unloading and the Marines were ashore with food and ammunition in short supply. The Navy did not have enough ships to stay and protect the island and the supply ships that had pulled back could not return to unload.

The First Marine Division was surrounded by the enemy. The Japanese on the island could be reinforced with men and matériel and could move around the Marine perimeter at will. Having just landed, the Marines had no fortifications, no air support, and no cover. General Vandegrift was forced to throw away the book and devise another strategy, which he did on August 9. The new orders: (1) Get the airfield finished. (2) Get the supplies off the beach, disperse them, and if possible, hide them. (3) Dig in along the Tenaru River, the eastern flank, dig in on the west along the ridges that abut the sea.

The third platoon led by Sgt. Morgan, Tee's DI from boot camp, set up their position on the ridge with a good view and field of fire. They assisted in stringing a strand of barbed wire and then dug their foxholes.

"McLauren, set your BAR here between Hinson and Smith," he barked, indicating Tee's Browning automatic rifle. "Smith will be on the right with his machine gun and Hinson on the left with his M1. Hinson, fix your bayonet on the rifle. McLauren, you and Smith keep yours handy along with your Ka-Bar knife. When they come, we'll open fire as soon as they get in the water and don't let up. Have your clips and magazines ready for reloading and use everything you have if they break through. There'll be a bunch of them so some will get through the wire. Don't leave your position because there is always a lot of confusion when it starts. Keep your heads." He went up the line squad by squad and then settled into a position where he could see and command.

The men set up on the west bank of the Tenaru River heard noises, but so had everyone else on the island. Then a badly wounded native came into the position with information of the force moving toward them. They struck at 0118 hours on August 21. A green flare rose from the opposite bank, casting a ghostly light over the sandspit. A Marine sentry fired a shot. Within minutes, several hundred Japanese came charging across the sandspit toward the platoon of G Company, reinforced with two platoons of Battery B, special weapons battalion, and the fight was on. The Japanese ran headlong into a single strand of barbed wire the Marines had strung and were hit by small-arms fire and canister from the 37mm cannon of the special weapons unit. They waved their arms and shrieked — but kept on coming. They broke the line of defense and for hours it was hand-to-hand fighting with small arms, knives and bayonets.

Tee and his squad opened fire effectively, but the enemy soldiers broke through the wire and were quickly in the defense line. Smith and Hinson were killed in the first wave and Tee fired the BAR until he ran out of ammo, then picked up the M1. He struck the first enemy soldier to reach the trench with the butt of the rifle, then the bayonet. He was followed by another, and then another who screamed and lunged at Tee. He shot some and struck others.

After a time it got quiet and Tee was able to reload his weapons and set out hand grenades as he waited for the next wave. It was then that he noticed the blood on his jacket and was able to put a bandage on his chest wound. Sarge was right; there was confusion and Tee couldn't see who was still with him, but the only thing on his mind was getting ready for the next wave.

Sgt. Morgan spoke out loudly. "Stand fast. They'll come again." Another green flare and the Japanese soldiers charged just as before except that there was no barbed wire to slow them down this time. Tee tossed grenades, fired the machine gun until the ammo ran out, then the BAR, and resumed fighting with the M1.

The strategic questions of who, when and how also apply to the man in the foxhole. They first called him the Japanese soldier, then simply the Jap, but Tee was engaged in hand-to-hand fighting and he saw him simply as "the enemy." Face to face, eye to eye, knife to knife: He felt him, and could even smell his breath. He was the thing that was trying to take your life and your job was to take his. Tee shot some, struck some with the butt of the rifle, ran his bayonet through some and each time he felt a sense of elation. He felt a kind of thrill; he liked it and later, upon reflection, he realized that he was a killer and was good at it. They had trained him to do it and he not only learned how, he excelled at it.

The reserve platoon helped stem the tide and this was followed with artillery striking their positions as they again massed to cross the river. At 0830 the First Battalion, First Marines crossed the river upstream and enveloped the attackers. Company C then closed in and bayonetted the survivors. The final count listed six to seven hundred enemy killed, thirty-four Americans killed, and seventy-five wounded. Colonel Kiyonao Ichiki, commander of the Japanese shock regiment, shot himself through the head after burning his colors.

Chapter 41

The Wounded

The wounded Marines were taken to a field hospital and treated for gunshot and bayonet wounds. Tee's wounds consisted of a wide but not deep bayonet slash across the chest, which required considerable stitching, and a cut across the left side of his face which was also stitched. He was confined to the hospital unit for several days. Sleep came easily from the exhaustion and as he rested he reflected on the fight and the fact that in the heat of battle he had ceased to think of the Japanese soldiers as people, and had seen them only as the enemy that had to be killed. They told him in training that you must hate your enemy and Tee was impressed at how easily he had come to that point.

When Tee reported back to his platoon his wounds were treated daily by the medical corpsmen and he took over his assignment as squad leader. Sgt. Morgan came by and commended him on his outstanding bravery. He also told him the commanding officer had recommended him for the Navy Cross, then presented him with his corporal stripes. He and his drill instructor were now fellow noncommissioned officers...*semper fi.*

Reflecting further on these events, Tee decided then that he would not try to keep in touch with his family or friends. He was what the Marine Corps wanted him to be, but now he believed that he would never return home. He would do his duty, which was to kill the enemy. He would perfect his squad and make them the best in the company. The question of "who" was answered, and he also knew the answer to the "when" and "how." He would kill them *when* they attacked him, and he would pursue them *when* they didn't. He would find them and kill them by any means available, which answered the *how* question.

It was far from over. The enemy was even more determined and was provided with more troops and supplies, plus very strong naval support. They had brought in long-range artillery and air power and subjected the defenders of the airfield to hourly attacks that destroyed most of the Marine and Navy planes and the runways. Men who are trained to attack find it hard to hunker down under fire and not respond and this is especially true with the leaders who set in motion a plan to attack and silence the big guns in the process.

Squad leader McLauren joined with the attacking units and again displayed his exceptional ability as a Marine. The respect he and his men shared was now increased by friendship. No longer waiting for the enemy to attack, the Marines sent out patrols to find and destroy them. Tee and his squad became especially adept at weaving their way through the heavy brush and muck and developed methods and techniques, which made them unpredictable and lethal. These successes led to another award for bravery, the Silver Star. He also accumulated two more wounds and two more Purple Hearts. He was the most decorated man in the company and the most admired. He also remained the most misunderstood, except for Sgt. Morgan, who not only knew him well, but was to a great extent responsible for why he was that way. They were both what the Marine Corps wanted and needed most of all.

What bullets and knives couldn't do, malaria did. Guadalcanal was a cesspool of almost every form of misery a person could be exposed to and Tee was no exception. Chills, fever and fungalinfections began to take their toll and the strong young man fell ill and lost weight and strength. From the 1,941 cases of malaria reported in October, the figures had risen in November to 3,213 and it was time for the First to have a break and rebuild what they had sacrificed in the four months of extreme exposure to warfare and disease. And so it was in December that General Vandegrift turned over command of the island to Major General Alexander M. Patch. The First Marine Division left the island.

General Vandegrift addressed a letter to those who had taken part in the Guadalcanal campaign:

"In relinquishing command of the Cactus Area, I hope that in some small measure I can convey to you my feeling of pride in your magnificent accomplishments and my thanks for the unbounded loyalty, limitless self-sacrifice, and high courage which have made those accomplishments possible.

"To the soldiers and Marines who have faced the enemy in the fierceness of night combat; to the pilots, Army, Navy and Marines, whose unbelievable achievements have made the name 'Guadalcanal' a synonym for death and disaster in the language of our enemy; to those who have labored and sweated within the lines at all manner of prodigious and vital tasks; to the men of the torpedo boat command slashing at the enemy in night sorties; to our small band of devoted allies who have contributed so vastly in proportion to their numbers; to the surface forces of the Navy associated with us in signal triumphs of their own, I say that at all times you have faced without flinching the worst the enemy could do to us and have thrown back the best that he could send against us.

"It may well be that this modest operation, begun four months ago today has, through your efforts, been successful in thwarting the larger aims of our enemy in the Pacific…"

The First Marine Division was moved to Melbourne, Australia, and the men were welcomed to the beautiful city. Their time there would be fondly remembered when they went back to their purpose, which was killing Japanese. Tee was recovering from his wounds, which didn't limit him very much, but the malaria did. Loss of weight along with chills and fever and the fungus-infected wounds were serious limitations and required constant medical attention, which placed him in the sick bay and under the watchful eye of Navy doctors and nurses. He became a special patient for one of the nurses and began the healing process rapidly under her personal care and attention, which extended to frequent visits after hours. She had access to transportation and together they made many Jeep rides into Melbourne.

Time and distance make a difference in relationships and Elizabeth's picture was stored in the footlocker. The nurse had come on to him and he had responded. The relationship was torrid but brief and then it was over. He thought about Elizabeth and reaffirmed his decision to break it off. No letters and no picture in the wallet. Whatever life he had would be spent in fighting and killing and it would be easier to do that if he was free of those things that give hope to the future. He planned no future.

Military units are welcomed into communities and, after a while, there are people who are glad to see them go as well as others who would like for them to stay. It was this way with the First and the time had come. It was a return to the jungle to continue the advance across the islands, pushing the Japanese back with new strength gained from the war effort at home, which brought new equipment and replacements. They also benefited from the knowledge gained from their Guadalcanal experience. The naval and air support were stronger and the ability of the enemy to reinforce their troops was curtailed; this contributed greatly to the success of the ground troops. Amphibious and jungle warfare were different and the First was good at both. Their confidence was high from the successes and they were pleased at the praise they were receiving from the home front. America was proud of the young men who showed the world that the American soldier was willing and able to confront any enemy.

Cape Gloucester in New Britain, near Papua, New Guinea, was a return to the constant rain and jungle miseries with hard-fought victories. It was the same as before: hand-to-hand and up-close combat. The enemy was committed to fight to the death and the Marines were committed to sending them there. When the flag was raised to symbolize the security of the entire Cape Gloucester area, it was drenched in the rain and hung limp as the men slogged away from the ceremony. Now-Sgt. Tee McLauren led his platoon to once again find a dry place to rest and recuperate. Sgt. Morgan had been moved up to the company level and Tee was his replacement. The foulness of the weather and the island infected the previous wounds and Tee once again was experiencing the ravages of malaria.

There was a widespread rumor that they were going back to Melbourne, but this was generated more from wishful thinking than actual information and it was a serious blow to morale when the men learned the rest and recuperation was to take place on another island named Pavuvu. It was the largest of the Russell Islands, part of the Solomon Chain, some sixty miles from Guadalcanal. Not much was known about it, but it looked good from the air with waving its coconut palms. It turned out to be just another hellhole.

It irritated the Marines that folks at home were of the belief that all of these islands were tropical paradises while they were struggling to rest in knee-deep mud and were drenched by constant rain. It was even too small for training exercises. Even those who were nervous about combat were not too reluctant to leave the place. Word came down that those with twenty-four months of service would be rotated home and among these were Sgt. Morgan and Sgt. Tee McLauren. Those leaving didn't celebrate openly out of respect for those who were staying.

1944

Chapter 42

War Effort

Patriotic spirit was high, and the needs of the war were being met at home by dedicated civilians working in factories and shipyards producing weapons and equipment for the armed forces. Other less obvious contributions were being made in offices, shops and other places where vacancies were created when men left to serve.

Miss Charlotte was teaching at the junior high school, Emily Masters was working in the supply department of the shipyard and Elizabeth was serving coffee and doughnuts at the USO canteen and striving to be nice and cordial while declining many invitations from a lot of good-looking young soldiers and sailors. Mary worked at the office of the dean at the College of Charleston, while doubling up on her courses in an effort to graduate early. Charlie was in England, and they planned a wedding as soon as he came home.

As a bomber pilot, Charlie already had thirty missions under his belt and was looking for a rotation home after twenty more. Daylight bombing was costly in both planes and airmen, and the prospect of twenty more missions was not something to take lightly. Men at war know the peril and the risks and they plan and are dedicated to it.

Elizabeth had no plans, but she had a picture at her bedside, and she spoke to it every evening. She had no plans but plenty of hopes. Her father, Captain Masters, was now Major Masters, and was serving in the Pacific. Elizabeth and her mother still lived on Rutledge Avenue, where they would have nightly visitations from young would-be suitors who, despite being discouraged by Elizabeth, still gathered on her porch…with diminishing hope.

Mannie Simmons was feeling his age and so was his horse. His cozy complex remained a good home to a big brown dog, a strange cat and a flock of chickens. The garden was productive, and he shared his produce with neighbors, including the widow of his late friend the Major. He could still find good seafood to go with the vegetables.

More than a year had passed since Major Frank Manigault had died quietly in his sleep. A day or night never passed that he didn't present himself in his widow's dreams or reflections and she could smile…even with tears in her eyes. She appreciated Mannie's visits.

Mannie still slept upstairs as before and, as before, late one night he heard the stirring around in the horse stall where a bed was being made on the hay bales. He wondered why Tee always came in the rain and was happy that he had.

After Guadalcanal there had been Gloucester and more of the same harsh, jungle warfare against a fanatical enemy. More malaria and jungle rot to go along with shrapnel, bullets, and bayonets. When it was time for Tee to come home, there were a lot of people anxious to see him. He had been dropped off on Chapel Street and had declined an offer of help to get out of the car, but he did accept help in finding the walking stick that had fallen on the car floor.

With a handbag in one hand and the stick in the other, Tee proceeded down the alleyway to the place where he had always found quiet comfort and friendship, which he needed again.

The brown dog nuzzled him as he entered the stall, as did the old horse when Tee fed him a handful of oats. The bales once again invited him as he fashioned his bed on the straw and pulled the old blanket over himself. Sleep descended over him and he found comfort he could not find in the super-nice beds at the naval hospital.

Mannie was up earlier than usual, knowing that his young friend was asleep in the straw and he could wake him up to another good Mannie Simmons breakfast. The coffee was on and the stove heating up when he heard the stirring of Tee getting into his uniform. Mannie walked to the stall to greet him, accompanied by his dog and cat.

"You always come at night and in the rain," Mannie said. "Do you bring the rain or is it just coincidence?"

"If I had control over the weather I would hire out to farmers and people like that," responded Tee. "I would charge big bucks!"

"How good it is to see you, Tee," Mannie said. "I'm sorry the Major can't be here to enjoy it with me. I'm sure you heard…I miss my old friend."

"Mary wrote me," Tee said simply. "I quit writing back because I thought I wouldn't come home and that it would be best to break everything off."

"We all worried about you, especially when you quit writing. We should have known that you would survive, but with no news we worried. Look at those medals! You are a real hero."

"I don't feel that way, but I am proud of my medals."

"Sit down over here and drink this," said Mannie, as he handed Tee the same old chipped cup with no handle. "I have a couple of things the Major wanted to pass on to you: his .45 automatic he carried when he was a soldier and a rare leather-bound book of essays by Ralph Waldo Emerson. I've been reading in it and it's not easy, but it's rewarding. He underlined some good passages. It's one of those books that it takes a lifetime to understand. You'll not only like it, but you will benefit from it. You take the book with you and I will keep the automatic unit until you can."

"Thank you, and I wish I could thank the Major for remembering me this way," Tee said, sipping the best coffee he had tasted in a couple of years. "I guess it's why I was drawn back here last night. Even this old cup is part of the magic of this place, the things that Major Manigault felt and what the two of you shared with me. The two of you helped pull me off the junk pile and I have never forgotten that." He looked happily into the smiling and dignified face of his most unusual companion. "I'm so sorry about the Major."

Mannie gestured to his young friend's legs. "Your wounds, the walking stick. How bad is it?"

"It's not permanent. In the jungle everything becomes infected and my leg is heavily bandaged, but it's healing. I'll be fine. My doctor said the scar on my face would make me look like a Prussian. I don't know any Prussians, but I think he meant it as a compliment."

Mannie chuckled. "The girls will love it, Tee, and speaking of girls, Elizabeth Masters is still in town but is being heavily courted by a lot of good-looking young guys."

"Fill me in on everyone," Tee said, changing the subject.

"Sit over at the table and let's enjoy some fried fish and scrambled eggs. I don't have any bacon; the pigs went to war too."

The reunion continued with a lot of small talk and smacking of lips as they polished off the seafood and eggs breakfast and Tee soaked up the magic of the unusual compound and residence of Mannie Simmons.

"Your daddy is back at sea but lives on the farm when he's ashore," Mannie said. "He has a lady friend. Everyone has someone except you, and you're being scoped out by a very pretty and popular young lady. Your daddy rents out the farm, except for the house, and still plans to retire there."

"He should," Tee agreed. "He should retire there. He should also have a lady friend and I'm happy for him. Tell me about Mary."

"Charlie is flying bombers out of England and they plan a wedding when he comes home. Mary is almost ready for graduation. She goes straight through summers and all and carries a maximum load. She is still someone special in many ways. She worries about Charlie and even more so about you. You have to see her today."

"I will, but not today," replied Tee. "I'm trying to readjust. I can't explain how I feel, even to the doctors who are trying to help. Time is a good healer and I have plenty of that now."

"I guess you're at the Navy Hospital. How long have you been there?"

"A week," Tee said. "I didn't want to be seen like this. The malaria has taken me down a lot but that's pretty much behind me. The leg thing is almost behind me; the big problem is my head. I don't know how to discuss it, and to be truthful, I don't want to. I want Mary to know I'm home and OK. Tell her for me and that I'll see her in a few days."

"You should do it yourself," Mannie insisted. "She's your sister and you should go and talk with her now. She's still at 28 Chapel and probably will just be getting up about now. Go do what we both know you should."

Tee was finishing his breakfast and took one more gulp of the good coffee. "You're right, and I'll go now," he agreed. "I don't want her to worry about me any more than she already has."

He left, after again thanking his friend for his hospitality. Mannie struggled with his feelings as he watched his young friend limp toward the street. *He is still strong and looks like a recruiting poster despite the malaria and the wound*, he thought. *He's a good Marine and has done his share of the fighting.*

Chapter 43

A Surprise Visit

Mary was fixing her breakfast when Tee let himself in. She dropped the spatula and stood frozen for a second and then raced across the room and embraced her brother. She noticed the scar on his cheek and her eyes filled up as she kissed it. Tee knew right away that Mannie had once again led him to do the right thing.

He explained to Mary why he hadn't come earlier and why he wanted to wait a while before meeting any of their other friends. Mary said she understood, although she didn't. Tee didn't stay long, explaining that he had left the hospital without notice and had to meet his ride back. Mary cried.

The scar on his face and the limp. She couldn't control her emotions and wiped her eyes continually as she walked to the college. It was more than just the things she could see; there were those things she felt and saw in his eyes. He was not well but he was home, and she tried to console herself with this.

After class, Elizabeth took Mary aside and demanded to know what was wrong.

"It's Tee," she replied, and before she could explain, Elizabeth said with panic in her voice, "Is he OK?"

"He's home…not home but in the Navy Hospital," she said. "I saw him briefly this morning and he's been hurt badly. He doesn't want to see anyone right now and he went back to the hospital. He has a scar on his face, and he is walking with a stick. He had malaria and has lost a lot of weight and is in a bad mental state, which is why he doesn't want to see anyone. He said he would come back in a few days."

Elizabeth felt many of the same emotions as Mary had and was torn between the joy of knowing Tee was back and the anxiety about his wounds. She had waited so long already, and if he was sick, she wanted to be part of the cure.

"I want to see him now and I will," she said to Mary as they separated. Mary went to her job at the college and Elizabeth to Rutledge Avenue, where a major in the Marine Corps had just arrived home from the Pacific.

* * * * *

Tee got back to the hospital in time for breakfast and his absence didn't cause any problems for anyone. Later in the day he was again seated in the mess hall when Major Masters slipped into the chair next to him.

"Keep your seat, sergeant," he said. "This is a social call but also a command performance under direct orders from my daughter and wife. You are expected at our house tonight at seven o'clock for dinner and you are to be in full winter green uniform with ribbons in place. You will be inspected by the women in charge of my household and I will be there to witness the proceedings and to salute a Marine who wears the Navy Cross. I'd rather wear that medal than these leaves on my shoulder. It's great to see you and to be home myself."

He said all these things with genuine warmth in his voice and a smiling face that Tee could not help but appreciate.

"What a pleasure, sir," Tee said. "I don't know how I came to be so blessed as to be home again and welcomed by such wonderful people. I'll arrange transportation and I'll be there."

"The transportation is already arranged. Just be ready when I come and pick you up. A Navy Cross, a Silver Star, and three Purple Hearts deserve special attention."

Tee replied, "I see among your rows of ribbons a Silver Star and a Purple Heart too. When my leg gets well, I'll chauffeur you around. In the meantime, you rate a salute." With that, Tee stood and rendered a snappy hand salute which was returned and followed with a warm handshake.

This exchange did not go unnoticed by those in the mess hall, who already viewed Tee with special regard. The quiet and reflective patient was capable of smiling and the medical staff was especially pleased to see what to them was progress.

Chapter 44

The *Mary Mac*

There were two pictures of the *Mary Mac*, one on the mantelpiece of the Rowland family, who were proud of their son, and one on the bedside table of Mary McLauren, who enjoyed seeing it as she retired for the evening and again when she entered a new day. She spoke to the smiling captain who was waving from the cockpit of the B-17 bomber he flew on missions over Europe who was also the one who had named it. She was the *Mary Mac*.

The B-17 was America's first four-engine, all-metal bomber and designed for high altitude, daylight precision strategic missions against German industrial and military targets. It had a ten-man crew comprising a pilot, co-pilot, bombardier, navigator, flight engineer/top gunner, radio operator, ball turret gunner, two waist gunners and a tail turret gunner. It earned a reputation for its ability to keep flying despite serious damage and its defensive firepower, becoming known as the "Flying Fortress."

On a mission in December 1944 the *Mary Mac* was filling the position in the formation known as "the hole," which was the last plane in the bottom group — and vulnerable. The crew experienced no flak or enemy fighters on the way in but met the usual flak over the target. It was barrage flak and accurate and rocked the ship. The bombs were released, and Charlie turned sharply to the right and, in flyer parlance, "got the hell outta" the area.

Even so, the flak continued to break all around the ship and Charlie felt the same as he had in every mission before: his pulse throbbed, and the sweat ran down his back and he felt hot and flushed. He always cooled down whenever he left a heavy flak area and the sensation brought on something akin to pleasure. It was a return to normality and pleasing to know that he could conquer fear. Suddenly, flak exploded and took several feet off the left wing and shook the *Mary Mac* violently. In addition to the wing there was a large hole in the body of the plane.

The American fighter escorts were engaged in a dogfight, leaving a gap that brought the German Focke-Wulf 190 fighters out of the clouds. They were firing their 20mm cannons, which were striking and exploding as they hit the ship. Equipment and other flying parts of the ship added to the shrapnel. Some struck Charlie on his feet and legs and badly wounded some of the crew. The cockpit filled with smoke and flames from exploding oxygen tanks; some of the gun positions were hit directly, killing the gunners.

The *Mary Mac* was mortally wounded, and they were flying at 20,000 feet. Charlie gave the order to abandon ship. Some of the crew who were able strapped chutes on those who were disabled and tossed them out of the plane. Charlie was the last to get out. He attempted a delayed jump and timed himself to open his chute at 10,000 feet. When the air filled the chute, the jerk snapped his body, the rushing air roaring in his ears stopped, and everything became quiet and peaceful. At first, he was able to see the chutes of other crew members, but the wind shifted, and he was blown some distance away. He was alone.

* * * * *

Hopes were high in Charleston that Charlie would soon be home, and the planned wedding could take place. Mary was close to graduation, which was a commitment she made that had to be accomplished before she could marry. The Rowlands were educated, and she wanted to fit into their culture, not so much for social reasons but simply to blend in. It was her idea alone and the Rowlands came to understand the girl who was not ashamed of tobacco stains on her hands.

December had arrived and plans for Christmas were starting to emerge when the devastating telegram arrived.

THE SECRETARY OF WAR DESIRES ME TO EXPRESS HIS DEEP REGRET THAT YOUR SON CAPTAIN CHARLES ROWLAND HAS BEEN REPORTED MISSING IN ACTION SINCE DECEMBER EIGHT OVER FRANCE STOP IF FURTHER DETAILS OR OTHER INFORMATION ARE RECEIVED YOU WILL BE PROMPTLY NOTIFIED STOP
THE ADJUTANT GENERAL

Mary was notified at her job in the dean's office and went immediately to join the family in their grief. She could only sit in the room with his mother and grieve quietly as Mr. Rowland struggled and tried to find something for them to seize onto to generate some hope.

"He's missing, he's not dead. A lot of airmen have been shot down and most of them survive. Charlie is strong and capable, and he would expect us to try to be the same. Pray. Pray for him and pray for strength for ourselves. That's what we must do." The stricken father said these things tearfully as he struggled in his efforts to be manly. Christmas was no longer in their thoughts.

The picture of the *Mary Mac* sat on the mantel and became

the focus as the days wore on. Charlie loved his plane and his crew, and they had returned time and time again from their missions and usually with only slight flak damage. It was different this time, but they all prayed and hoped against hope that he would return.

Chapter 45

Torn

It was a Friday afternoon and Mary sat at home on Chapel Street after attending classes and working at the office of the dean. She wrapped herself in a blanket and from her seat on the porch, despite the tears, she could see the traffic on the Cooper River while she struggled to deal with her widely divergent emotions.

She was happy for her brother but concerned about his physical and mental conditions, his mind more than the other. Tee was always strong and still had that working for him, but he kept his thoughts to himself and shut others out when it came to his emotions, but at least he was home.

Charlie was never out of Mary's mind and she struggled to keep her thoughts of him positive. War changes everything and everyone and she had not only seen it, she had experienced it. She was so deeply submerged in these thoughts she failed to notice when Elizabeth came up the stairs and tapped her on the shoulder.

"Oh, hey!" she said with surprise in her voice. "I didn't hear you come up. Get under this blanket with me and let's study the river together," she added as she shifted into a different and more receptive mood. "I'm glad you came. I've been in a slump all day and need good company."

"I thought about you all afternoon. You showed it in your face: wanting to be happy for Tee and worrying about Charlie. I thought you might need a shoulder."

"I'm trying not to let myself go into mourning over Charlie. I have high hopes that he will make it back and, at times, confident that he will," Mary said. "I need to spend more time with the Rowlands, but his mother is so consumed with grief and his father and brother are trying so hard to console and assure her while trying to conceal their emotions that I don't know how to conduct myself when I'm there. It's hard, but I'm not going to break down and sob until there is proof that he has been killed and, if that is the case, I'll share her grief. I'm trying to believe that he will make it and trying to get comfort from that."

"That makes sense, and you always do," Elizabeth assured her. "Life has not been easy for you and you have developed a toughness because of it."

"I wouldn't call it toughness. I have a faith and rely on it to lead my life," Mary replied. "I know that life is not easy for most people and they must know how to go up a hill or down a hill and stay on their feet. You don't want me to go into the difficulties of our lives, but we are a closer and wiser family because of them. Adversity makes you examine everything, and you become a better person if you do it right. I'm trying really hard to do that."

"Speaking of your family, I plan to be a part of it soon," Elizabeth said. "Tee and I are getting married."

"When did he ask you?" Mary asked, surprised.

"He doesn't know it yet, I haven't told him, but he's spoken for and engaged even if he doesn't know it," Elizabeth replied. They laughed and the mood was changed. Tee was home and getting well and the two friends sitting on the porch were happy. Mary had always wanted a sister.

"When do you plan to let him know?"

"No hurry. He's comfortable at our house and fits in well with my family. He has Dad's respect, mostly from the ribbons on his chest and the scar on his face. The Navy Cross is a high honor and the battle scar adds to it. Dad is filled with the *semper fi* and we're a Marine family. Tee has found his place in the world and it so happens that it's our world too. I'll fill him in on the marriage in good time."

"You've been raised in 'Officer's Country.' How do you feel about joining the 'rank and file'?" Mary asked curiously.

"You know the answer to that. I'll be happy with him wherever he is," Elizabeth said. "I knew it the first time I met him. He's one strong man but clever women have always known how to deal with that. No. He won't get away. Another thing, my dad started out as an enlisted man and earned a commission and he believes Tee can do it too."

"Really?" Mary asked. "What can your father do to help him?"

"Dad is talking with some contacts at Quantico and Officer Candidate School," Elizabeth continued. "I don't think he's talked to Tee about it and it hasn't come up in any of our conversations, but I heard him tell his contact that Tee was the ultimate Marine with proven ability and courage. He also talked about his lack of formal education but said that Tee was bright and quick to learn. I'll take him just like he is, but I want him to be a lot more because he has shown that he is capable and that he deserves it."

"Ha! Ha!" Mary laughed approvingly. "You're one of a kind and will make a good sister. Right now, I'm going inside and make some coffee for my good friend." As she rose to her feet, Mary added, "I don't imagine that the Marine Corps is looking for pure academics, but an officer candidate has to demonstrate the ability to understand complicated things and to solve difficult problems. Even without formal education they can test for aptitude and they certainly know how to train their people. Tee would make a great officer. Men will follow him…but let's go get that coffee and get ourselves warm."

* * * * *

The next morning found Mary bustling around the apartment and preparing to spend the day with the Rowlands. They would appreciate some help in the kitchen and other household chores, and it was her intention to take care of these things while avoiding the pall of grief that had descended on the house after the telegram about Charlie being missing in action. Tea and sympathy were not in her plan, but grits and eggs and toast were.

She arrived early and went straight to the kitchen. It wasn't long before the men were with her sniffing the bacon and smiling at the cheerful girl wearing the apron and the big smile. They were seated and enjoying the meal when the doorbell rang. A telegram delivery boy stood outside.

They knew what it meant. News! The question was what kind of news and they hesitated before going to the door. Mr. Rowland slowly moved to answer the doorbell and took the telegram. It was not from the Army Air Force, but from Paris.

IN PARIS SAFE STOP WILL SHARE DETAILS LATER STOP REJOINING UNIT IN ENGLAND STOP WILL CONTACT YOU SOON STOP LOVE CHARLIE

Emotions ran high. There were tears, smiles, hugging and laughing — and even dancing by a delighted and restored mother, father and brother. Mary joined in the tears and smiles, and she too laughed when Mr. Rowland lifted her from the floor and spun her around to the delight of everyone. It's amazing how joy can so quickly erase sadness and the more the sadness, the greater the joy. It was a great day and the page was turned.

Later they would learn how Charlie landed in a clearing in the woods after drifting into Belgium and was hiding his parachute when a young man came through the heavy brush and gave a friendly wave. He took the chute and assisted Charlie through the woods to a cabin, where he had him wait while he got an interpreter and some medical help for his feet and legs. When the help arrived, the news was good. General Patton's army had advanced through the area and the enemy was gone. That was one item of good news. The other was when the medic treated the wounds; he found them to be painful but not serious. The trip home had begun.

Charlie's rescuer left him in the cabin while he went into the village to an American Army unit where he informed them about Charlie. An Army jeep was quickly dispatched to bring him in. A certain amount of questioning took place to make sure Charlie was truly an American airman but the parachute and his dog tags along with his wallet full of pictures took care of that. His wounds were treated more thoroughly by another Army medic and he found himself in a convoy headed to France. When he reached Paris, he sent the telegram home.

After a couple of days in Paris, Charlie was on a flight to England and headed to a reunion with his outfit. Although they were scattered over a wide area when they bailed, most of the other crewmen survived. The exceptions were the gunners who were casualties from direct hits before the *Mary Mac* went down. They did what all combat soldiers do: they rejoiced with the survivors and honored the others with raised glasses and shared memories of their pals. Sometimes these stories would bring gales of laughter and sometimes moments of quiet sadness. A man lives if he is remembered, and they would never forget.

More medical attention took the pain out of Charlie's wounds and with some bandaging he was fully out and about but without a plane. Replacements were plentiful now and his days over Germany were over. He wrote letters home and made a phone call that found Mary at her desk at the college. "Make the arrangements," he said simply. "I'm on the way home."

The dean found her with her head on the desk. She responded quickly when he spoke to her and she wiped her eyes and presented a happy face as she told him the news.

"Go home, Mary," he said. "You won't be any use to anyone today and this is not where you should be on a day like this."

Mary had affection for the courtly scholar and this act of kindness and consideration was another reason to appreciate her good fortune in moving from the cigar factory to the refinement of his office.

"Thank you, sir," she almost shouted as she left the office, taking the steps two at a time on the way down to Calhoun Street.

He watched her graceful exit and thought how wonderful youth is and remembered it was why he took his job in the first place. Her pretty, happy face had been transformed into true beauty by her tears. *Powerful things, tears. They make a happy face happier and a sad face sadder*, he thought as he walked back into his office.

Sometimes you can't wait to share good news and at other times you simply want to quietly let it soak in. Mary chose to go back to her seat on the porch on Chapel Street and enjoy the view without the tears this time. To her surprise she was greeted by her brother who was in her glider swing and taking in the view himself.

"Charlie called and he's on his way home," she said after a good embrace. She took her seat beside him.

"Great news! I see a family get-together, or rather, a get-together of our enlarged family," Tee said, adding, "I also see a wedding."

"Whose? What plans do you have?"

"Elizabeth and I are getting married when I get back from the Pacific," Tee said. "I expect to ship back out right away. The Japanese are losing every battle in the Pacific but have shown no intention of quitting. The next step is Japan itself and it will be the hardest. Street by street and door to door. They didn't just ship their fanatics to the islands, they feel the same way at home and seem to welcome dying. Major Masters will be going back too. Elizabeth knows these things."

"When did you discuss marriage with her?"

"She doesn't know it yet, but she won't get out of the trap," said Tee as he looked at his sister and laughed.

"So, you set a trap. Have you ever heard of getting caught in your own trap? You may not be the clever hunter you think you are."

"You think she's smarter than your brother?"

"How do you imagine that women have been in charge of the world so long? They're smarter than you and your pals. God gave men muscles and women brains," Mary laughed back at Tee. She was pleased to see her brother moving from his mental retreat back into her world.

SPRING 1945

Chapter 46

The Rowlands Wait

The big plane touched down at Charleston Air Base and the tired passengers were escorted to a barracks where they could sleep the rest of the night. It was close to four o'clock in the morning. when Charlie was able to get to sleep and he slept soundly until he was awakened at ten. He hurriedly dressed and caught a ride into the city.

The Rowlands were all on full alert and greeted him with great joy and pleasure when he came in. Mary was in the kitchen and was standing in the doorway, smiling and waiting her turn. Anxious mothers have a firm grip on those they love and it's even stronger when danger is involved so it was not easy for Charlie to go where his eyes had been focused since he came in. They met in the middle of the room and once again Charlie was caught in the strong embrace of a woman in love.

"We're going to have a conversation with a preacher tomorrow," Charlie whispered softly in her ear.

"Miss Charlotte called and invited us over tomorrow afternoon for a welcome home party. She has invited our friends and we just must show up. Five o'clock," she said.

It was an hour before Charlie could get Mary by the hand and slip away and continue his conversation about the preacher. There was no hesitation this time and the next morning the two of them were in the office of the Second Presbyterian Church planning a small wedding.

* * * * *

Tee arrived on Judith Street an hour before the reception and was welcomed on the porch by the gracious lady. They sat in the rockers and sipped iced tea and munched on snacks. A strong emotional tie bound them together, this mother with a lost son and this son with a lost mother. They supported each other by filling these voids and the separation and wounds of war added to the deep satisfaction generated by the simple act of reunion.

"Let's talk straight," said the gentle lady. "You are home but different from when you left. That's natural. What war doesn't destroy it changes and you left as a strong young man and now you're a strong young man with a lot more maturity. Elizabeth has been loyal to you even though you didn't ask her to be. There are a lot of disappointed young men who knocked on her door while you were gone and all they got in return was a warm smile and polite rejection. It's your move."

"I know. I plan to marry her if she will have me and is willing to wait until I get back from the Pacific. The big move is yet to come, and I will be a part of it. Japan. We will invade them and defeat them at home. They will fight and a lot of people will die. I might be one of them, so I'll ask her to wait."

"You must do more than that. You've got to stake your claim, as they say out West. Take this and put it on her finger," she said as she handed him a diamond solitaire ring long in the family that had been intended for the bride of her son. Again, Tee was moved to tears. The kind and gentle little lady on Judith Street had the key to his emotions.

"How can I accept so much from you when I have given so little?" he protested. "You saw through me immediately. A thief. I used the word 'teef,' but I was a thief and you were among the first to know. Now this ring. I can't accept it."

"You must accept it," she countered. "Don't you understand how much you helped me? I love you like the son I lost, and you made it back from the war. You're a part of my family and I want her in it too."

"She'll be here, and I'll bend the knee and we'll see. You have been so kind to me, and I can never repay you," he said while holding Miss Charlotte's hand and looking away to give his eyes a chance to dry. She smiled and was happy.

A few minutes later Mannie Simmons arrived with a bottle of single malt from the Manigault collection and Miss Charlotte went inside and reappeared with shot glasses...three of them.

"Well," said Mannie, "we are being honored."

"Don't be so surprised, these old lips have sipped a lot more than iced tea. Here's to your health," she proposed as she joined the men and emptied the glass with a grin and chased the drink with the back of her hand.

"Women. They never cease to amaze me," said Mannie. "Did you see the way she threw that drink down? Like a sailor." He grinned. "They play with us like a cat plays with a ball of yarn."

The other guests began to arrive, and Miss Charlotte greeted them, suggesting the men continue to enjoy their reunion alone in the side yard garden with its wrought-iron table and chairs.

"I might have another with you later, but Miss Charlotte gave me a ring and it wasn't intended for my finger. One drink is enough to give me the courage and another might twist the tongue," Tee said, rising to his feet. "I'll be back for the other later." While walking away, he was looking over his shoulder and exchanging grins with his wise old friend.

It was easy to get Elizabeth away from the others when she came in. She went straight to Tee and took his arm, then led him to the opposite end of the porch and out of the sight of the other guests. It also was easy to get to the point.

"Miss Charlotte said she gave you a ring," Elizabeth said.

"So, she told you."

"Yes, a week ago. You might as well accept the fact that while you are a good Marine you need to go to charm school to keep up with me. We women have the social equivalent of the *semper fidelis*. It's that thing that enables us to remain in charge while allowing you to think that you control the world. Now, what are we going to talk about?"

"Let me catch my breath while I struggle to 'take charge of this situation' as they say at Parris Island. You need the strong hand of a Marine to lead you down the path of life. I mean, another Marine. Your folks did a great job with you, but I intend to pick up where they left off. I want to put this ring on your finger, and I want you to promise to wait for me until I get back from my next tour."

"Tee, I've loved you from the time we met. I want to wait for you as your wife. If I lose you the pain won't be any easier to bear if we are not married. I'm from a Marine Corps family and I want more than anything to be your Marine Corps wife."

"Will you marry me?" Tee asked, as if it had been his idea.

"I'm not sure," she replied. "This is such a surprise." And then they laughed.

Whatever doubt may have existed was gone when they embraced in a new and wonderful way, forgetting about the party and the other guests. It was a struggle to come back to earth, but they managed it, walking arm in arm back down the porch and returning to the garden, where more of the guests now gathered. Miss Charlotte was waiting and grinned openly at the now obviously engaged couple locked arm and arm and wearing the glow that only complete happiness can give. There was a lot of handshaking and backslapping along with hugs and kisses before Elizabeth joined the ladies and Tee was able to break away to rejoin his friend at the wrought iron table.

Tee accepted another glass of single malt. Mannie was pleased and amused. "Put your head in the noose, didn't you?" he chuckled.

"With pleasure. I'm not sure what happened. I was not in charge, that's for sure. What surprises me is how easily she takes charge. It must be a Marine Corps thing. She takes over like a drill instructor, but with silk gloves. I know that I'm not stupid but she's always ahead of me, even the proposal. It was like she posed the question and she already knew the answer. It should scare me, but it doesn't. Oh, hell! I'm a brave Marine."

"You're a willing victim in the greatest game of life. You like it that way. Here. Drink up. To your future, it sure does look good from here."

Miss Charlotte came out on the porch and called everyone inside. "Let's all raise our glasses," she said when they had gathered in the dining room. "We have three returned heroes here, men who put it all on the line for us and our country. With their chests full of ribbons, they represent the best we have. I propose a toast to Major Phillip Masters, Captain Charlie Rowland, and Sergeant Tee McLauren…Hear! Hear!" she said loudly as she raised her glass.

"Hear! Hear!" came the lusty response from the party.

"Now, another toast. Wedding bells!" The guests roared and raised their glasses in happy approval as the two couples were brought out front smiling.

Tee shared the moment, accepting congratulations and praise, and then went back to the little table in the side yard where Mannie and Major Masters were remembering Major Frank Manigault with each sip of the Scotch. The subject turned to women.

"Our job is to fight the wars and their job is to take charge of our lives and move us around like some kind of board game," said Tee. "I proposed to Elizabeth at the time and place exactly as Mary, Miss Charlotte and Elizabeth had set it up weeks ago. I love it, but it's a little scary."

"You're getting wise. A man with a Navy Cross who fought a determined enemy hand-to-hand and knife-to-knife finds out that he is putty in the hands of the women," said Major Masters cheerfully. "It's OK, Tee. It works to our benefit because they would fight the same way for us. Just enjoy it."

The three men took another sip and raised their glasses in toast. It was a grand day, leaving everyone happy.

Chapter 47

The Last Interview

The interviews were coming to an end, as were a lot of things, including the war. George Johnson, the young reporter, made his way down the alleyway for the last time and felt a sense of regret. He had succumbed to the magic of Mannie's place, just as others had.

"Let me feed the chickens today. I never thought that I would miss seeing chickens, or a horse, an old dog or even an aloof cat," he said as he reached for the bucket sitting in the stable and began to scatter the corn around, much to the pleasure of the birds. "I'm afraid you have changed my life."

"Not really," Mannie replied. "I didn't change your life. Our lives change every day with our new experiences. You were put in contact with the simple life and now realize how pleasant it is. Chickens cluck their appreciation while they scratch and eat and it's a happy sound."

"True, and dogs are amazing. They attach themselves to us and show us real devotion."

"It looks like you have found the secret of my life," said Mannie, his contagious grin lighting up his face in a way George had come to appreciate. "They will stay with us even when we mistreat them and still find some way to make us happy. I would never mistreat a dog, but a lot of people do…Let's get down to business."

Mannie sat down and stared at the ground as he reflected on the things he wanted to say. This time the reporter would take notes while Mannie put his thoughts into words.

"This is an extremely eventful time," he said. We lost our president, Franklin Delano Roosevelt, when he died on April 12 at the Little White House in Warm Springs, Georgia. He served us for twelve years, making him our longest serving president. We don't know much about our new president, Harry Truman. Most of what we do know is that he was in the haberdashery business in Missouri and is not a very impressive-looking man. But he did serve in the Great War as a combat soldier, and that means a lot to me."

"Well, Germany is through, so the challenge now is Japan and we know we can beat them, but we don't know at what cost," said George.

"The loss of American lives is the ultimate cost. It becomes more than statistics when we know some of them as friends and family. Tee is like family to me and he has proven himself to be a good Marine but sometimes the brave ones are the easiest targets," Mannie said in a soft voice, and with a solemn face.

"This is my last assignment," George said unexpectedly. "I'll be eighteen next week and I signed up. I'll leave for Parris Island a week from Friday."

"Well, that makes it more of a concern for me than before because you are someone else for me to worry about now," Mannie said. "VE Day was a joyful time and in celebrating we were able to take our minds off the war in the Pacific, but that is behind us now and we can't afford to take anything for granted. Iwo Jima and Okinawa made it clear that our enemy has lost none of his fanaticism and attacking the homeland will be even more difficult."

George said, "You're right about how things change. On May 8 when Germany surrendered it was celebrated in Europe and America, but millions had been killed and Europe will be permanently changed. Britain had heroically borne the brunt of the war but would no longer rule over an empire where 'the sun never set.' Now it will be our turn."

Mannie nodded and asked a question that had been raised when George told him his age. "How did you get the job of a reporter at seventeen?"

"I was the editor of the high school paper so I had some experience and besides, there's a war going on, you know, and they had to take what they could get," said George, and they both laughed.

Chapter 48

Back at Parris Island

Tee was at Quantico and, to no one's surprise, he was approaching graduation. His letters to Elizabeth reflected his confidence in his ability and his happy anticipation of their upcoming wedding. Major Masters was at Camp Lejeune as a part of the build-up for the invasion of Japan. He read with great interest the letters from home detailing plans for the wedding.

June came and the newly commissioned Marine Corps second lieutenant strolled down the alleyway to Mannie's home with a smiling young recent college graduate on his arm. A week later Mannie was seated in the sanctuary of the Second Presbyterian Church with a small group of devoted friends witnessing a unique ceremony. Two ceremonies, to be exact. Tee and Elizabeth were married immediately following the wedding of Charlie and Mary. He wished very much that his old friend Major Manigault could have enjoyed it. A wedding is a beginning, but old things are remembered even when they come to an end. Friendships live on.

"I've got thirty days of leave and then I report to Parris Island as a range officer. Elizabeth and I are taking a trip to Florida for a honeymoon, but I'll see you before I report," Tee said to Mannie and several other well-wishers who had surrounded the bride and groom.

"Is the assignment permanent?" Mannie asked.

"No," Tee said with a grin. "I think my father-in-law arranged an extended honeymoon for us, but I'll be back in the Pacific soon, and so will he."

The ceremonies were unique but simple and Mannie had a greater appreciation than most of the others because he remembered the wild young boy who had climbed on his wagon and forced his way into the lives of himself and his good friend the Major. The walk back to Chapel Street was warm with memories of his two unusual friends.

It was almost a month before Tee showed back up at Mannie's. He had brought something for his friend and his friend's dog and cat, but there he drew the line. As he explained to Mannie, he was stumped by the question, "How do you shop for a chicken?" Mannie liked that line.

"I'm reporting for duty tomorrow and I'm glad to be a Marine again," Tee said. "Rifle range duty will be fun, and I can find housing on the Island and see how good Elizabeth is at homemaking."

After a long visit over cups of Mannie's special coffee, his host said, "We say goodbye a lot these days, but so far you have always come back. I don't need to tell you to be careful."

* * * * *

The Jacksonville bus took Tee back to Yemassee and a shuttle bus onto Parris Island, where he reported for duty just as he had as a raw recruit. Transportation was provided for the trip to the range where he would work and be quartered until he made other arrangements for his new bride. Tee stepped off the bus and found the headquarters building, where he threw down his seabag and reported in.

"I'm being assigned here, and these are my orders," he said. "Who's in charge?"

"I'm still in charge here, lieutenant," said a familiar voice. It was Gunnery Sergeant Morgan. "You don't need to stand at attention this time," added the former drill instructor and Tee's first Marine Corps teacher, as well as his leader in combat.

"Salutes, handshakes, hugs — I don't know which way to go, but what a surprise!" Tee said. "You will always be my teacher, sergeant."

"Bars and medals. I don't need to teach you anything. I always knew that you were a special Marine," Morgan said. "The Marine Corps is my home and yours too. This is where we belong." The gunnery sergeant was speaking from the heart, proud of the man he had a hand in making.

"Let's enjoy this duty while we can, because we both know where we are going — and soon," Tee said. "I want you to meet my wife and watch you wonder how this 'gravel agitator' managed that. She's as much Marine Corps as you or I. You'll like her."

Tee spent a few hours with Sgt. Morgan checking out the target frames in the pits, reviewing the training regimen and, finally, being driven over to the bachelor officers' quarters where he was assigned a room while he waited for married officers' housing to provide a home. Not much had changed since he had gone through the training depot because the basic training for a Marine is to be a rifleman. He can go from there, but he'll still be a rifleman.

Soon Elizabeth arrived and they set up housekeeping in a

small house on the base. The month of July went by quickly and happily. Tee liked his work and Elizabeth liked their house. They didn't talk about shipping out or invading Japan; they loved being alone in their new home and were even more thrilled by a doctor's report.

"Boy or girl? Which do you want?" asked Tee.

"One of each," replied his happy wife. "You know I don't care. I just want a good, healthy child and a father in the house. I couldn't be happier. We're a happy and growing family and I feel confident in our future even in the face of the things to come."

Chapter 49

Endings and Beginnings

The war continued while its political and military planners considered various strategies. The Japanese, who had conquered part of China and shared the vision of world conquest with Germany and Italy, were now pushed back to their small island and committed to a fanatic fight until death. Those planning the invasion of Japan were concerned with the loss of more American lives and adopted the same strategy Germany had used against England: Surround them and starve them out.

Strategic bombing of military installations was replaced with incendiary bomb attacks on the civilian population. It was very effective against homes which were generally flimsy and flammable. Then, on August 6, 1945, the world was introduced to a new horror: the atomic bomb.

Hiroshima was devastated with an immediate killing of 70,000 people, to be followed by countless others who would die from the after-effects of radiation. Three days later Nagasaki suffered the same horror, with an immediate loss of 50,000 lives with more to follow. The demand for unconditional surrender was accepted and the war ended. There would be no costly invasion, but instead a peaceful occupation. War changes everything and this was never so true anywhere as it was in Japan.

Tee and Elizabeth found even more reason to celebrate their life together with the threat of more combat removed, at least for a while. After six months on Parris Island, they were assigned to Camp Lejeune, where Tee became a platoon leader. The role was easy for a Marine who had been trained for the role from inception: from a private in a squad in heated combat to a squad leader, then a platoon sergeant and now a commissioned platoon leader. He had no trouble getting respect. When he appeared before his platoon with a Navy Cross, a Silver Star and three Purple Hearts on his chest, the respect was immediate. Even in fatigues and without the ribbons there was the combat scar. His men obeyed his orders without question and his fellow officers were pleased to be his friend and comrade.

The Masters family closed their home on Rutledge Avenue when Mrs. Masters joined her husband in his new assignment at Camp Pendleton in California. Elizabeth and Tee settled into comfortable quarters at Camp Lejeune and were joined in April by a healthy baby boy. It was September 1947 before Tee took leave for a trip back to Charleston.

They walked down the alleyway, a proud Marine with a boy on his back and a pretty woman on his arm. This time it was not raining, and it was daylight. Mannie was up and about when the big brown dog rose from his place close to the stove and stood wagging his tail, announcing company. Mannie came out of the shed to greet them.

"Mannie Simmons, meet Mannie McLauren," Tee said.

"You named him Manigault?"

"Of course. We couldn't pass up an opportunity to honor two

people who took a young punk off the junk pile and led him into a wonderful life."

Tee put the boy on the ground, and he tottered over to the big dog and patted his head. Then the little one turned to Mannie and was lifted and received into the magic place. Coffee was served in chipped cups with broken handles and Tee extended an invitation from Miss Charlotte to Mannie. "She said that you must join us on Judith Street this evening. It promises to be a fairly large gathering of happy friends, and she said that she will provide the Scotch," he said. "The Rowlands, Mrs. Timmons and Essie, Charlie and Mary, Major and Mrs. Masters. Even my father and his new wife, and a lot more friends. She wants you to join her in a toast so she can once again show you how to belt it down!"

Mannie accepted the invitation and watched the little family walk back up the alleyway as he sat alone in the shed. Mannie stroked the brown head of his old dog and reached for his treasured pocket watch to check the time. He turned the watch over to once again enjoy this gift from the Major's estate. The inscription MANIGAULT on the back always reminds him of their great friendship. He spoke softly to the devoted face of the dog: "Yes…we really miss our old friend."

Being alone never bothered Mannie, as he loved to use such moments to reflect over past times, and this led him into a mental conversation with his old friend, Major Frank Manigault.

Some say that God doesn't have a plan for us and doesn't intervene in our lives. I don't agree and you don't either. We are called on to make a lot of choices in life and are expected to make them, but a wise man prays for wisdom to make the right choice for the right reason. I watched that boy we knew and worried over walk up the alleyway with his family and felt like you were watching too and felt the same sense of wonder. We saw the changes take place in his life and we know how remarkable it was for him to not only survive the most dangerous combat, but to emerge from it a hero, and it was something to see him with his family.

It's when you look back at life that you see God's hand. I've been struggling to understand the way the war ended. The big bomb. Tee struggled with his feeling of what he thought was pleasure after killing the enemy in hand-to-hand fighting. He came to understand that what he felt was not pleasure but relief from being the one to survive.

I wonder how it feels to kill thousands with one bomb. I hope they can see it as having done their duty...but it's different. I wish you were here to help me answer these things. I sure do miss my old friend.

★